THE WOMAN IN THE CHIMNEY

Samuel Fleming

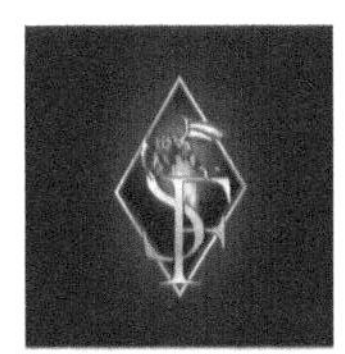

Contents

CHAPTER 1

Michael inched forward through the crawlspace and tried to ignore the crickets chirping around him. Tried not to think of the ones crushed beneath him, crusted into the fabric of his coveralls. He didn't enjoy killing them, but the little bastards gave him the willies.

His headlamp flickered in the dusty light, and he stifled a cough.

At least this house had a vapor barrier—the plastic scrunched beneath Michael as he crawled, sending a few more spider crickets to their untimely death.

How did anything live like this? How did he live like this?

"You see it yet?" Colton yelled through the floor.

Michael crawled forward, following his boss's voice, and muttered a curse to whoever put the panel on the opposite side of the house from the crawlspace access. Sweat beaded on his forehead.

"What was that?" Colton asked.

"Not yet!" Michael shouted. Just a little further—he hoped.

He pulled a length of coaxial cable and wire behind him, unspooling it as he went. One day they would have robots that could haul lines under a house, but until then, Michael got paid twenty bucks an hour to do it.

Most days it beat sitting in a cubicle or going back to school. Other days...

He came to a rise in the dirt and squeezed through the narrow gap under a floor beam.

Tapping sounded around the corner—on the floor above. His boss thought tapping on the floor with his pliers helped Michael find his way, like some goddamn sonar or something.

What it really did was annoy the piss out of him.

Michael called out, "I'm almost there." Keep your panties on, he added silently.

Finally, mercifully, he came to the ass end corner of the house where power came through the floor. There was already a brand-new hole through the subfloor waiting for Michael's dusty cables. He rolled onto his side and fished them up one at a time.

"Ah, there he is!" Colton said. "How's the view down there?"

"Next time, I call the attic."

"*Next time,* he says—we're leaving you down there, kid."

Michael barked a fake laugh and shuffled around to begin the long crawl to get out from under the house. At least now he could take his time; the longer the crawl, the more work the old man would finish by himself.

It was the spiritual successor to the impromptu bathroom break when work needed to be done, and, at the moment, Michael felt vindicated in using it.

Above, his boss grumbled as he connected wires to the breaker panel. With any luck, the job would be finished by the time he got out from under the house.

Then Michael heard scratching from behind him.

He rolled over and turned to face the direction of the sound, headlamp illuminating another corner of the crawlspace. He followed the dusty plastic waves of the vapor barrier, searching for the source of the noise.

It sounded like a cockroach or a wood bee, but it also sounded loud enough to be a mouse. As Michael listened, his boss fumbled with the panel upstairs and a tool scraped across metal—that wasn't it either.

The light of his headlamp rolled over the crawlspace, searching.

Michael stopped, his light highlighting a long, thin *thing*. It could've been a loose wire or a piece of trash, but in the harsh light beneath the house, it looked like a finger. Splotchy pink and gray.

His heartbeat quickened, and Michael swallowed the lump in his throat.

It was just his eyes playing tricks on him, Michael told himself. This wasn't the movies, where some creepy monster was lurking in the basement, waiting for the first unlucky electrician's helper to wander downstairs. The old lady who lived in the house wasn't some serial killer who stuffed the bodies of her victims in the crawlspace—

How would she have even lugged a body this far? Michael had trouble just crawling by himself.

Then the finger twitched and Michael's eyes went wide. Twitched, and then he heard the scratch again.

Subconsciously, he inched backward along the vapor barrier, making sure his light never left the finger.

Michael hit his head *hard* on the joist.

"Shit," he muttered, reeling forward and clutching his head. He winced and cursed again as he fumbled with his headlamp.

When he finally got the light situated, he glanced toward the corner of the crawlspace where the finger *had been.*

It was gone.

Michael redoubled his crawling and his cursing—this time careful to squeeze under the floor joist. When his belt caught on the beam, he grunted and pushed harder, finally slipping through the narrow gap.

Scratching.

Reflexively, Michael rolled and looked to the side. Sweat burned his eyes, and he blinked furiously. His light flashed across the crawlspace in time to see something disappear behind a block of the foundation. Something thin and pink and gray—

Something following him.

The plastic rustled, the thing tugging at the vapor barrier as it followed him.

Michael turned and crawled as fast as he could, kicking up dust and crushing crickets beneath him. He coughed and squinted, eyes watering, not daring to look back.

A high-pitched squeal sounded, and Michael rolled to his side, tucking his arms and legs for whatever was coming to get him.

In the dusty light, a big black rat darted past, its long, gnarled tail trailing behind it.

Michael shook and finally relaxed, cursing the nasty bastard, before he finally crawled the rest of the way out from under the house.

MICHAEL PUSHED HIMSELF TO his feet and stood in the sunlight, catching his breath. A breeze whipped by—chilly compared to the stuffy confines he'd just escaped from.

Finally, he chuckled to himself and shook his head. "You got me," he muttered to the rat, who wasn't listening. "Got me good."

Michael turned and walked around the edge of the rambler. He skirted the many bushes and flower beds that lined the edges. The rambler was huge, by single floor standards, and it felt even bigger now that he was walking around it to get to the side door.

When they'd pulled up, Colton had offered to take the attic work at their next stop if Michael did the crawlspace. Of course, Michael hadn't known how long of a crawl he'd just signed up for.

Like most things in this job, Michael vowed not to make the same mistake again—once was acceptable. Twice, and you deserved it.

Michael wiped his shoes on the mat, then opened up the sliding glass door.

"There you are," Colton called. The old man peeked out from behind caterpillar eyebrows and the door to the fuse box. "Was beginning to think you got lost in Narnia."

"I should've asked for directions," Michael replied, stepping inside and sliding the door behind him. His boss didn't reply.

He glanced around the lady's kitchen. It was orderly in a cluttered-grandmother sort of way. Gnomes littered the house. Whether they were sculptures or dishes or pillow covers, the little bastards were everywhere. In the kitchen, gnomes appeared alongside strawberries and mushrooms, seeming like they both lived in them *and* ate them.

Reminded Michael of his own grandmother's house, except she'd liked her football.

"She's got rats," Michael said idly.

"Oh, they don't eat much," Colton replied. Then he muttered, "Crap... Hey, I need you to go back under there."

Michael grit his teeth.

Then his boss peeked over the door with a wrinkled smile. "Just kidding."

MICHAEL LOADED UP THE work van while his boss went over the work with the lady of the house. He didn't mind, though. Sure, the toolboxes weighed a metric shit-ton a piece, but it beat talking to people.

Especially since Michael had already heard the lady talk his boss's ear off when they first got there.

Somehow Colton didn't mind. The boss could talk to anyone. Didn't matter where they were—inner city or in the sticks; didn't matter who they were—rich, poor, or thinking of themselves as firmly middle class.

He'd always been like that. Twelve years Michael had worked for him, and boy could Colton talk.

Michael locked up the back of the truck, then let himself in the front passenger door. He turned it on, rolled down the windows, and blasted the AC.

"Goddamn rats," he muttered.

Michael pulled up the address for their next job, then texted the office to confirm they would be on their way soon. Just as he was about to close his eyes for a minute, Colton opened the driver's side door.

There was no use in trying to doze off now.

"All done. Who's got two thumbs and is ready to go up in an attic?" Colton pointed enthusiastically at himself. "This guy."

"Alright, *Dad,*" Michael replied sarcastically.

They turned around in the driveway, and Michael watched the house fade into the distance. The old lady watched them from the window, becoming little more than a silhouette before they crested the hill.

Surprisingly, his boss didn't say anything else until they were out of the neighborhood.

"Hey, uh... Is something on your mind?"

Michael glanced over. His boss was side-eyeing him; his bushy gray eyebrows wrinkled and waiting for an answer.

"Just tired," Michael lied.

"It's just that you've been awful quiet lately."

"You do enough talking for both of us." It came out harsher than he meant.

"Awful jumpy too. On edge."

Michael scoffed.

"How long have you known me?" Colton asked, clicking on the blinker.

"Twelve, thirteen years," Michael replied.

He slowed to a stop at the light and turned to Michael. "And you still can't talk to me about stuff that's going on?"

Michael bit his tongue. In truth, Colton was like family to him, but it wasn't like Michael talked to his family much, either.

"You *depressed* again?" Colton asked. The words rolled off his tongue like he was pronouncing a different language—not condescending, but a struggle nonetheless.

"No."

"Cause you should do something," Colton went on. "Last time it was being a thirty-five-year-old helper. The time before that was a girl. The time before *that* was another girl. Then school—"

"Hey, *Dad*. You can stop helping."

"I'm just saying that those are all things you can do something about. They aren't going to fix themselves—sure as shit not if you just stay home and watch TV..."

Mercifully, his boss trailed off. Michael saw the old man glance dejectedly in his direction as traffic started up again.

Michael closed his eyes, and soon traffic was replaced with music as his boss turned on the radio. Oldies—the only shit they played this far in the sticks.

At least it was better than getting talked at.

Cause Michael sure didn't know how to talk about what was eating him.

CHAPTER 2

MICHAEL PRETENDED TO SLEEP the rest of the way home.

He felt the turns into the neighborhood, felt the bumps and pothole that marked his street. Then the work van stopped in front of his house.

He kept pretending to be asleep.

"Well, we're here," Colton said.

Michael made a show of waking up, yawned, and hopped out of the truck. He shut the door and looked at his boss.

"Same time tomorrow?"

Colton scoffed and raised his eyebrows, as if to say something, before finally letting it go. "Same time, same channel."

Michael waved as his boss drove off, then turned and walked to his house.

It was a short walk across the driveway. He scuffed the cracks in the pavement with his boot, drug his fingers along the hood of his old Pontiac that needed an oil change, and ignored other things that needed attention: The sidewalk, the gutters, a fallen piece of siding—a dozen other little things and a few projects to boot. Himself, too—throw him in there too.

Once he got inside, he briefly acknowledged that he should clean. Shit, his mother would've beat him if she saw the cobwebs he'd let grow in the corners. He grabbed a Coors from behind the old takeout, then walked past his dusty chimney and promptly collapsed in his chair.

The little rambler had been his childhood home. When he and his sister had grown up and got "real jobs", Mom had moved out and left him the place. She figured that Ellie didn't need the house—her and Darryl already had a bigger one—or the money, for that matter.

That was how Michael wound up living in his empty childhood home.

He glanced around for the remote before finding it in the crook of the chair. It never went far.

"What's on my mind?" he muttered to himself.

He turned on the TV and booted up apps to find a movie.

How was he supposed to explain just how much was on his mind?

Then, bitterly, he said to himself, "More like, *what's wrong with Michael now?*"

After all, what did he have to complain about? He had a house. Had a car. His job was alright—pay could always be better. He had dates, occasionally. Friends that he called every few months. Sister and brother-in-law half an hour away. Mom was doing alright.

But as the list dwindled, Michael knew the truth:

Counting his blessings never helped fill that discontent.

"Sorry, Ma," he muttered.

He flipped through random movies before settling on an old 80s action flick. Something mindless. Then Michael had another beer before making himself a microwave dinner.

He showered and went to bed at nine o'clock—he had to be up at four in the morning to get ready for work. Same shit, different day.

He laid in bed for an hour or so, flipping through social media and then opening the *Chances* dating app. It'd be nice to find someone local, but every time he had that thought, Michael would swipe to a girl he went to high school with—one that didn't age well—and he'd keep going.

He did have a match—Trina. Short with dark hair. On her profile it said she likes foreign films, NASCAR, and having fun. He cringed and sent a message to her asking what she was up to this weekend.

Michael laid back in bed and sighed.

Tomorrow was Friday. He could make it one more day. And who knew, maybe Trina would be interested, available, *and* their ideas of fun would mesh.

Maybe Colton was right; maybe Michael just needed to get out of the house. A date and a girl would take his mind off of things.

Or maybe it wouldn't. Maybe all those problems and the feelings would still be there when the date ended or when Monday rolled around...

How could he explain to his boss that he was just tired—damn tired. Of everything. Of *trying*.

Could always be worse, Michael told himself. At least he didn't want to off himself this time.

He just felt like shit.

MICHAEL WOKE UP THE next day, shaking off a dream about bricks and a chimney... or maybe it was another crawlspace. *Shit*, he couldn't even escape from work when he was asleep.

Immediately though, he cracked a smile. Trina had messaged back *and* she was free tonight.

Maybe things were looking up after all.

THE SUN WAS JUST starting to come up when Colton came by in the work van to pick him up. The old man was peering through squinted eyes and sipping on an oversized travel mug of black coffee. Michael got in and told him the good news.

Colton patted his shoulder. "There you go. Get some inertia, a little Trina—hey now, hey now. Don't slap a man while he's trying to drink his coffee."

Michael relented and stifled a laugh. "The last thing I need is you jinxing me."

"Fair enough," Colton replied. "My boy needs all the help he can get!"

WORK PASSED QUICKLY ENOUGH. Two jobs. Michael went up in the attic of the first house and the basement of the second house. Thankfully, he didn't see any more rats, not even any crickets, just cobwebs. But he couldn't shake that eerie leftover feeling of not being alone while he was in those spots.

Which was absurd. The attic and the basement were some of the cleanest he'd ever seen, cobwebs included.

Colton got off his back too. Good news about Michael's weekend seemed to put his boss in an even better mood.

The old man did not stop talking—all day.

The weather, random stories as a young man that Michael had already heard before, former jobs, and—thankfully—an extremely short-lived political detour.

"Don't go preaching to me," was all Michael had to say, and that was the end of it.

At least the Colton talking made the day go by quicker.

At the end of the day, Colton dropped him off and said, "Just put me on the phone if you can't think of something to talk about. It's called a *pinch hitter.*"

He didn't know much about baseball, but he knew that one. Michael got out of the van and called back, "Heard it before."

HE HAD THREE HOURS to kill before his date with Trina, so Michael set to cleaning.

Well, *picking up.*

He wasn't exactly betting on wanting her to come back with him—hence the current state of his house—but a man could hope. And he sure as shit didn't want her reviled enough to turn around before setting foot in the door.

He washed the two pots that perpetually stayed out, then did the dishes. He vacuumed the living room, kitchen, and bedroom. Then he set to cleaning the bathroom.

Then Michael shaved, showered, combed his hair, put on a nice collared shirt and slacks, and went to dinner.

MICHAEL MET TRINA AT *Joanna's* up the road. It was a little dive bar dressed in neon lights that did karaoke on Tuesdays, or at least they used to. Michael couldn't remember the last time he'd went. Their chicken fingers were good.

Michael grabbed a high table near the door. Then he waited, grabbing glances at the TVs playing games he didn't care about. He tried not to look as nervous as he felt.

Had it really been that long since he'd had a date? ...Since he'd been out?

He ordered a Budweiser and waited.

Trina showed up in a modest black dress and leather coat. She was actually much prettier than her photo, which made Michael feel even more nervous. His photo on *Chances* was two years old, and though he didn't like to think that he'd put on a few pounds since then—he had.

They exchanged pleasantries, and Trina ordered a Michelob.

Then they went through the motions of asking about each other's profiles and interests—stuff they already knew but wanted verified.

"Do you *indeed* like NASCAR?" he asked, trying to make an obvious joke about it.

It didn't land.

"I grew up watching with my dad," Trina replied. "You're not the first guy to grill me on it."

"Oh, that's not... I don't know anything about it, really. Fast cars are cool. Do you and your dad's cars ever compete?"

Turned out that she and her dad liked the same car—number forty-seven.

And that was how the evening went, Michael trying to hide the awkwardness he felt and constantly convinced that he was failing. Jokes didn't land, and eventually he quit making them. Instead, he asked about Trina, trying to appear interested instead of nervous.

She'd gone to the neighboring high school a few years behind him, so that helped—not that they cared about the same sports. He'd been a fan of the *Dog's* football team; she'd been a fan of the *Charger's* basketball team.

She was divorced from her high school sweetheart and not looking for anything serious. Michael tried not to linger on the fact that he'd never been married and made up a fake long-term girlfriend.

Trina wanted kids. Michael honestly didn't know if he cared one way or another and felt damned no matter how he answered. He settled on a tepid yes, which he swore she saw right through.

Memories of his last date came cringefully back to him. In a time when everyone could have just about anything on demand, he felt reduced to a checklist.

He *almost* swore she was nodding along with each of his answers, mentally crossing things off.

When a lull finally came, he ordered a second beer. So did Trina.

And Michael turned the conversation toward something lighter. Back toward her love of foreign films.

He didn't know shit about foreign films either, but he was glad to keep her talking. Anything to take the focus off of himself.

Finally, Trina's face lit up with a beaming smile. She told him all about how she got into them because of her college roommates, and there was something just *so different* about foreign films.

"It's almost like once you've seen one American film, you've seen them all," she said.

Michael listened as intently as he could because the other part of him was trying to think of the next question to ask: What were her top three favorite? What was the strangest, most out there one she'd seen? Which did she recommend for a newbie?

For the first time since the beginning of their date, Michael found himself smiling. Her enthusiasm was infectious. He really did want to know more about Trina's foreign films, even if he was far too nervous still to commit any of her answers to memory.

To see the contrast in her excitement, it almost felt like she tolerated NASCAR in comparison, like she enjoyed it only because her dad enjoyed it.

Michael never got the chance to ask her about it, though.

Trina smiled and shook her head. "Look at me going on and on. What about you? What do you plan on doing with your electrician *stuff*?"

The transition caught him off guard, and Michael felt like he'd lost control of his car on a rainy day.

Thirty-five-year-old helper.

"Well, uh, work's steady. I'll probably be with the company a while longer. No reason to rock the boat, I always say." Something he did not, in fact, say. Ever. His dad might've said it once.

"Okay," Trina said with a straight face. "What about you? What else do you do for fun?"

"Oh, well work's been real busy lately." Then he awkwardly tried to remember the names of *any* of the movies he'd seen recently—and failed. Even the ones he'd watched a million times.

It wasn't so much the nervousness that got him—it was shock. The slow realization that he didn't have anything that remotely interested him like the way Trina had gushed over foreign films.

It felt like looking in a mirror the morning after a bender or like seeing a plot twist for the first time.

Michael trailed off, then pretended that his phone was vibrating. He made a show of checking it, then mumbled a vague excuse about needing to go.

"Okay," Trina said. That was it.

Michael didn't give her a chance to say anything else. He felt awkward enough for the both of them.

CHAPTER 3

MICHAEL WENT HOME THAT night and fell asleep alone on the couch with movies playing in the background.

He woke up Saturday morning with a big notification on the TV asking, "Are you still watching?", and a message from his sister, Ellie.

Ellie 8:45 AM: *Mom's house sold. Need you to come by and pick up some things.*

He rubbed his temples and sighed. It was about time—Ellie and Darryl had been trying to sell it for almost two years.

Michael 10:15 AM: *Be by in a few.*

He got up, made a half pot of coffee. Then he ate a quick breakfast and prepared himself to go through the rest of his late mother's stuff.

MICHAEL WALKED OUT THE front door with a travel mug full of coffee and was nearly bowled over by the sun.

"Wow, Michael, late night, my man?"

Michael peered through slits in his fingers and saw his neighbor Felipe leaning on their chain-link fence. His accent was so thick that Michael came out like *Miguel*.

Michael smirked and walked toward the fence, stopping just short.

"Something like that," he said. "What are you working on today?"

Felipe gestured to the rose bushes lining the house. "Just pruning them. Anna is in there rearranging furniture. So I'm out here—*avoiding it*. You know what they say, no fury like a woman when a man is in her way."

Michael smiled, even though he wasn't sure if anyone else actually said that. Of all the neighbors on their street, Felipe was the one he actually talked to... on occasion. It helped that he was right next door, and always seemed to be outside working on something: Fixing the stairs, planting flowers, changing oil. He worked for a union in the city. Anna worked nearby as a front desk clerk.

"So, Michael, where are you heading?"

"Oh, we sold my mom and dad's old place. Going to finish cleaning it out."

Felipe nodded. "That's good, man. Glad your sister won't have to worry about it anymore. Plus, you electricians, you know, you get soft from that easy work."

Michael chuckled and waved him off. "I'm going to let you get back to avoiding your wife."

"Hey, just while she's rearranging the furniture!"

Felipe was alright by Michael. In many respects, Felipe was his closest friend. He certainly talked to the guy more than he talked to his old buddies.

MICHAEL DROVE UP THE road to his mom and dad's old house—their second house. The one Michael hadn't lived in.

By the time Michael graduated high school, his sister was already out on her own. When he got the helper job working with Colton, Ellie had already gotten married and bought a house.

Mom and Dad had decided to move as close as they could to Ellie and Darryl, thinking that they'd have grandbabies soon. It didn't matter how many times Ellie told them it wasn't happening, Mom and Dad still clung to their hopes.

They never brought it up to Michael.

He wasn't bitter about it, on account of not being set on having kids of his own, but it still stung.

Michael tried not to think about it as he turned onto their street, drove past Ellie's house, and stopped at Mom's old place. It was a proper colonial, something she'd been proud of. Dark blue siding with white wrap-around porch and shutters. Mom would've been proud of how Ellie and Darryl had kept up with the place.

The front door was open, and Michael could see someone moving through the screen door. Michael got out and walked up the porch and let himself in.

Michael stopped short inside. The immediate room used to be one of those *sitting rooms* filled with chairs that no one actually used—now all of Mom's old green flowered chairs were gone and the room was littered with boxes. Her old paintings were gone too, dust still marking their positions on the walls.

The kitchen was much the same—table and chairs replaced with a couple of boxes.

Michael looked around in disbelief.

The bathroom was the only room so far that looked untouched, but even it was missing some of the stuff.

Footsteps sounded behind him, and Michael turned to find his big sister staring at him expectantly. She was almost his height, but had somehow avoided much of the weight that had found Michael. She wore her "painting clothes" and her hair pulled back.

"What took you so long?"

Michael shrugged. "Didn't get your text until I woke up." He gestured around at everything already packed up. "What do you need me for, exactly?"

"We're going to take some stuff to the donation place on Marshall street. And we still need to go through the stuff in the attic—that's the bulk of it. You can still pick stuff up and put it down, right?"

Michael ignored the joke, and said in disbelief, "I just... remember her having more stuff."

Ellie shrugged. "Mom got rid of some things when Dad passed. We got rid of some when she passed. Don't you remember?"

He nodded absently. He did—it just hadn't occurred to him how many things had been piecemeal'd away.

"What?" Ellie asked. "Did you want any of Mom's furniture?"

Michael shook his head. Mom and Dad had basically furnished his house with their old stuff.

"No. Just show me what to start with."

Ellie turned and led him through the house, but not quickly enough that Michael didn't see a flash of annoyance on her face.

He let it go, or tried to. It was turning out to be a standard interaction between the two of them; Michael felt like he had to walk on eggshells to keep his big sister from being annoyed at his very existence.

They walked to the garage. Once it had been a two-car garage—before their family moved in. While Mom and Dad lived there, it had been packed to the brim with enough tools and storage bins so that only one car fit.

Now, it too was surprisingly empty. The rows of metal shelves were bare, picked clean like the ribs of some enormous carcass. Power cords and light fixtures hung from the ceiling like entrails.

In the center of the garage were a dozen boxes, piled together like a sacrificial offering of cardboard and packing tape.

"This is all the boxes from the attic," Ellie said. "Darryl and I haven't had time to go through any of it yet. And..."

"What?" Michael asked.

"It's probably sentimental stuff. You know, the kind that *family* should look through together."

"Darryl's family."

Ellie sighed and pulled a pair of box cutters from her pocket. She handed him one. "I'm talking about *us*. You and me... Let's just get this over with."

Ellie was right. Most of the boxes were heirlooms. There were two boxes of old photographs. Some were from when Mom and Dad were little, but the important photographs had been put in albums and already moved to Ellie and Darryl's house. Most of the photos from these boxes were from extended family, and labeled vaguely as photos of Jerry, Linda, Anne, Mikey—if they were labeled at all.

"Shit," Ellie muttered. "We might be able to figure some of these out. Darryl and I can go through them later. Compare them to the others in mom and dad's albums."

There were another two boxes of war memorabilia. Their great-great-grandfather had fought in World War I. His helmet, badges, and empty clips were in one box. Dusty uniform and flag in another.

"You should have these," Ellie said.

"Okay," Michael replied. Honestly, they would just be going from one attic to another, but maybe he could find a nice display case for the flag. That seemed like the right thing to do.

Another two boxes were full of cards from birthdays and holidays. Their grandparents had started the tradition, and apparently Mom and Dad had kept it going. Michael offered them to Ellie.

Lastly, was a box of newspaper and odd trinkets. A small carved elephant, antique medicine bottle, and pressed and dried flowers.

Michael had been about to write off the box when Ellie stopped him. She'd found something else as she dug through the newspaper and held it up proudly.

"Do you know what this is?" she asked.

It was a ring. Tarnished gold with a small ruby in the center. Tiny diamonds had sat around it, but several were missing.

"Grandma's old engagement ring?"

Ellie smiled warmly and earnestly. "The very same." She handed it to Michael, and he turned it over gingerly in his hands.

"Why didn't Mom ever wear it?" he asked.

Ellie shook her head. "I'm not really sure. At one point, Mom claimed she lost it, but then later she claimed it didn't fit. She never went to get it resized or fixed though."

"Weird. It's a nice ring. Definitely needs to be cleaned up."

"You should have it," Ellie said.

Michael looked at her, wondering if she was joking. "I'm not going to wear it."

"You dork. Get it cleaned up and then you can give it to someone."

He chuckled awkwardly. "You have to find someone first. Are you sure you're not getting ahead of yourself?"

Ellie folded her arms across her chest. "I'm not taking it. You hold onto it."

Michael rolled the old ring over between his fingers again. She wasn't *wrong*; he might find someone to give it to one day, but he felt bitter just holding the thing. Old feelings of resentment and dejection welled up in his chest, which he quickly shoved down and tried to forget about. Just like before.

"Michael…"

He looked up and again found sincerity in his sister's eyes. It was a feeling he'd been missing, and he didn't know for how long. It took him back to when they were younger and whispered secrets to each other after their parents went to bed.

"I know you've had hard times," she said, "but don't be bitter. We're not meant to be alone."

Michael nodded along. He wanted to argue, wanted to say that he'd made it this far on his own just fine, and that it was getting harder by the day to imagine getting as lucky as she and Darryl had gotten. But he didn't. Michael stayed silent and nodded.

Then he pocketed the ring.

Chapter 4

THAT NIGHT, MICHAEL FELL asleep in his reclining chair, empty beers sitting next to him and TV on.

He dreamed he was on a date.

Michael was out at dinner, laughing, and smiling so much his cheeks hurt.

He looked over and saw a woman sitting next to him, her hand resting on the table—cautiously close to his. She was maybe a few years younger than him, her skin a beautiful pale. She was wearing something like a white sundress. Long dark hair half-hid her face.

She flashed a smile—Michael felt that she was smiling a lot, and it put him at ease.

But she never spoke. She listened intently as Michael talked—at first about work, then about an embarrassing story from childhood where he'd run out of the house without pants on.

She laughed, a quiet and wheezing one.

Michael turned back to the cooktop. Both of them were the only two sitting around a stovetop at one of those

Chinese cook-in-front-of-you places. The chef was dousing the stove with onions and oil, and carrying on about something—putting on a show for them.

But Michael was only half paying attention to the scene. He kept sneaking glances at his date—

And she kept glancing at him, smiling and looking away when their eyes met. It was like she was peeking out at him from behind dark curtains or a veil.

The chef pulled out a long lighter and lit the oil, which flared up in front of them.

The heat was intense—Michael winced and leaned back in his chair. His awkward smile faded a little.

The girl was still beside him, and hadn't flinched at all. If anything, she was staring even more intently at the display in front of them. The fire reflected in her dark eyes.

Michael was still recoiling from the heat, which had grown and felt blisteringly—painfully—hot. He cried out for the chef to turn off the stove, but then the heat abruptly stopped.

The cooktop disappeared. The chef and the restaurant disappeared.

They were back at Michael's place, standing at the front door of his childhood home.

She pushed open the door excitedly. Michael didn't remember unlocking it.

She turned back to look at him, her long dark hair still concealing half her face. She smiled and pulled him forward by the hand.

But Michael was no longer smiling. No longer happy.

His heart was pounding like it was about to leap out of his chest. His throat felt like it was seizing up and he couldn't breathe.

He was scared. Terrified.

Of Her.

Of letting her into his life. Taking her to bed.

His knees felt weak and numb as she led Michael to his room, her grip cold and hard around his wrist. Painfully tight.

He struggled, and she dragged him.

MICHAEL WOKE IN HIS reclining chair, gripping the armrests like he was about to fly off of it. He shivered at the cold sweat that had soaked through his shirt.

His heart was still pounding, and he wiped his face with his hand—not sure if it was sweat or tears.

Across the room, something scurried up the chimney.

Michael stared at the bricks, frozen.

It looked long and thin and pale, like a spider's leg. Which was absurd, because it was far too big. Maybe it was a squirrel that had come down through.

Michael waited and listened, trying his best not to make a sound, breathing as quietly as he possibly could.

He didn't hear anything. No scurrying. No scratching. No chittering.

It wasn't until his forearms started to cramp up that he realized he was still gripping the armrests.

Michael released the armrests and sighed, laying back in his sweat-soaked chair.

It had been a long time since he'd had a nightmare, especially one that felt so damn real. Then again, it had been a long time since he'd remembered his dreams at all.

Michael laid there and closed his eyes. Despite laying in his own cold sweat, he was so exhausted that in moments he drifted back off to sleep again.

THE NEXT MORNING, MICHAEL got up groggily and started the long process of waking up enough to mow the lawn.

Michael felt the ring pressing into the front of his thigh; He'd forgotten about it. He took it out and placed it in the top drawer of his dresser. It was as good and as safe a place as any for it. He would get a nice case for it sometime.

It was almost 11 o'clock and three cups of coffee before he made it outside. It felt like it took another eternity for his eyes to adjust.

Felipe was already in the yard, gassing up his own lawn-mower.

Michael shook his head. Their family must've already gotten up, went to church, and come home. He really was dragging today.

"Michael, my man," Felipe called out with a wave. "You trying to race today?"

Michael forced a laugh. "Compete with a master? Never."

"How do you think you become a master, eh? Practice."

"By practicing *after* you've woken up."

"Man, you're crazy—hitting the sauce again."

Michael hesitated. "Bad dream this time, actually. About a girl."

Felipe walked over to the fence and leaned on it. "It's got you pretty shook, eh?"

Michael nodded and felt slightly ridiculous. He was already standing near the fence, about to talk to his neighbor about a bad dream. Michael *hated* listening to people talk about their dreams—it was almost as bad as listening to someone tell a story that a friend told them that none of those people weren't actually present for—a third-hand story.

Hey, listen to this thing that I think is interesting that didn't actually happen to me. It happened to Dream-Me, but also, it didn't actually happen.

Yet, here he was, already spilling it out to his neighbor and—God bless Felipe—he actually feigned interest.

When Michael was done recounting the dream, Felipe nodded along.

Michael asked, "What do you think that means?" It wasn't quite a rhetorical question.

Felipe shrugged. "There might be a reason for it. Maybe your date you just went on, but you want to know my take? ...It's all random: Dreams, life, weather. There's no rhyme or reason to any of it."

Michael's forehead wrinkled. "What are you talking about? Science can explain the weather."

Felipe wagged a finger. "Yeah, but they can't predict all of it. There's still a lot of random. That's why people fall for conspiracies, you know. They want—no. They need to believe that things happen for a reason. The government's incompetent, the government is run by lizard people? ...Nah. The government's incompetent. That's all.

"Look, here I am talking your ear off. You're distracting me so you can cut the grass faster!" Felipe laughed suddenly and turned back to his lawnmower, leaving Michael alone at the fence.

FELIPE FINISHED HIS LAWN first, which wasn't a surprise to Michael. He imagined it wasn't a surprise to Felipe either.

Michael finished mowing and trimming the lawn, then he started the washing machine and took a much-needed shower. He had a few beers while prepping lunches for the week. Like most weeks, this involved making meat and cheese sandwiches, and setting aside fruit or something like granola bars to snack on. Sometimes left-over take out took up a day.

It was a mindless task, the perfect kind for a Sunday. Michael listened to his 2000s rock playlist on his headphones while he worked.

He worked until he saw something out of the corner of his eye—something by the chimney.

He had the shades drawn, and his single overhead light was weak, so the living room was a little dark. He stopped and turned off his music, intently watching the chimney.

But he didn't see anything move again.

Michael shook his head. Maybe he was going a little crazy. Maybe he needed a break. His boss had joked that he needed to take time off; maybe Colton was right.

Then again...

Michael set his headphones on the table, then walked over to the chimney.

The light switch was on the other side of the room, but he could just use his phone flashlight.

Michael turned on the light on his phone and knelt down on the cold bricks. Light played over the chips and divots like the stone of some old cave. It was an odd thing, in that regard; the chimney didn't match the house at all. The house was small and fairly remodeled, but as far as Michael could tell, the chimney was *old as dirt* and seemed like it had never been fixed up at all.

He leaned over and shined his light up the chimney, leaning over progressively farther and farther to get a good view. Until he was nearly twisted around on his back.

Michael followed the bricks up and up, past bits of insulation and mildew—

"Shit," he muttered. He craned the light upward and found more insulation.

He had a heat pump, so he'd never needed the fireplace. Michael had forgotten that they had stuffed the chimney full of insulation. He wasn't even sure when the last time Mom and Dad might've used it.

Now the insulation was ragged, wet and green with mildew. Some small animal had probably torn bits of it out to line its nest with or was still currently nesting in the chimney itself.

Michael sighed. There was another project to do.

One that could wait for another week.

Michael pushed himself up and went back to making his lunches, doing his best not to think about what might be sharing a house with him.

CHAPTER 5

Michael dreamed about Her again Sunday night.

They were out in town, standing on the sidewalk while a river of obscured faces passed around either side of them. The sun beat down overhead, oppressively hot and stifling.

"Where are we going?" Michael asked.

She brushed aside a strand of her long dark hair. She was beautiful, and Michael melted a little at her smile. In that moment, he didn't care where they were going, as long as she was going with him.

She smiled coyly as she pointed over his shoulder.

Michael turned to see the banner declaring, "Ice Cream! Ice Cream!"

They walked over together, Michael shielding his eyes and desperate to step into the shade.

Thankfully, the line was short, and moments later, they were both standing under the overhang. When his eyes adjusted, Michael looked at his date, and found her staring at him with an intensity that startled him. Her dark eyes were half-hidden behind her hair, but she stared at him, unblinking, like she was staring into his soul.

Michael tried to ask what was on her mind, but his throat was dry and scratchy—his voice completely muted.

Meanwhile, she just stared at him, unblinking.

Michael turned and looked up at the menu, which was blurry and unreadable. It didn't matter, though; he already knew what he wanted.

He always got plain chocolate. Sometimes he'd get hot fudge, but only when the mood struck him.

He tried telling this to the cashier, a faceless young man, but he seemed to already know what they wanted and handed them two cones.

Michael took the chocolate cone.

His date took the other one that looked like it might've been strawberry or cherry—pink cream with chunks of red.

The line was long behind them, and they were forced to step back out into the hot sun. Michael shielded his eyes and took measured licks of his chocolate cone. It felt impossibly cold contrasted with the Summer sun, but it was already melting and starting to drip onto the sidewalk.

He savored the taste and spared a glance at his date.

She was slowly licking her cone. Each tiny lick somehow both proper and seductive. Michael couldn't help but stare out of the corner of his eye, missing his own cone twice.

She met his eyes, and suddenly he felt ashamed of staring. But she only smiled and pulled her hair back over her ear so he could see her better. Pink and red dripped down her fingers and onto the pavement.

Michael was vaguely aware that his own cone was dripping, all the while he snuck glances at his date while she licked around her ice cream.

As he watched, his stomach began to turn. Michael looked at his ice cream, thinking that he was getting food poisoning, but it tasted just fine.

He turned back to his date and watched as she licked the cone—

Her tongue wrapping nearly around it.

Around and around.

He stared, unsure of what he was seeing, and it was a long moment before he realized that her tongue was too long to be human. It slithered and wrapped its way around the cone like a snake.

His dread grew as her tongue extended. A shiver ran down his neck and shoulders. Then the soft touch of a whisper in his ear.

Michael jolted awake, arms pulled tight across his chest. He'd made it to bed this time, but still managed to sweat through his shirt.

Instead of going back to sleep, he got up and turned on his bedroom light and looked over the room. The sheets on the bed were twisted, half hanging off, but otherwise everything was where it should be.

"Shit," he muttered. He wiped the sweat from his face and waffled between trying to go back to sleep or just getting up.

The clock read three in the morning.

Michael shook his head, pulled on a new shirt, and walked to the kitchen to make coffee.

On the way, he stopped to turn on the light in the living room, if only so the damn house wasn't so dark.

The living room looked the exact same too—empty beer cans laying on the end table beside his chair. He'd clean them up later.

It was a ridiculous thought—it was just a dream. He was alone in the house. He was always alone.

Then he heard a soft tapping that sounded like it was coming from the living room.

Michael inched forward, listening intently, and after a moment, realized that it was the sound of water dripping. Very slowly. The noise was so faint and he didn't want to drown it out with creaks from the floor.

Michael turned to the old chimney, his eyes lingering there.

Sure enough, he saw a tiny drop on the dark bricks.

Michael groaned. That was just what he needed. He knew the chimney needed work and probably needed to be repacked with insulation to keep out the chill, but he'd hoped that it was sometime in the distant future. A problem for future-Michael—not for him.

He had enough sense to know that if it was leaking, then it was likely filled with mold and God knew what else.

He walked over and stooped down beside the bricks. There was a tiny puddle forming in the center, where logs might've been. Dark water on dark brick.

Frustratedly, he reached out and wiped a finger in the puddle. It came away tinged with black.

"Shit," Michael groaned again. That was just his luck. He stared at the puddle, frustration boiling inside him until it was borderline anger, before finally getting up and storming off to the kitchen.

He flicked on the light and started a pot of coffee. He grabbed a plastic container and brought it over to the living room, cursing again as he set it under the chimney.

Then Michael sat in his chair and waited, shaking his head and muttering while both the coffee pot and the plastic container filled with black liquid.

MICHAEL WOKE UP TO his Monday morning alarm. Even with a cup of coffee in him, he'd dozed off in his chair with a movie playing.

He groggily got ready for work and waited for Colton to pick him up in the work van.

"Rise and shine, Sleeping Beauty," Colton said, taking a long drag from his mug. "Happy Monday."

Michael sighed.

It was going to be a long day.

THANKFULLY, MONDAY CONSISTED OF routine checkups. No installs or maintenance.

On one hand, the work was mindless.

On the other, the day dragged on until Michael felt like he was stuck in purgatory.

Colton was content to talk Michael's ear off as they drove between houses. The old man had spent the weekend with an old friend—drinking and fishing, fishing and drinking. The hum of the engine undercut everything.

"You must not have drank that much," Michael said. "You're too cheery."

His boss laughed. "I drank enough for both of us. I just handle it better than you. Do you... Do you want to talk about your folks' place?"

Michael had mentioned going through the last of Mom and Dad's stuff, but had kept it at just that—a mention.

"Not sure what there is to talk about," he replied, watching the shops pass by.

"I don't know. I just remember what it was like going through my pop's place after he passed. Felt empty. Hollow. Felt like I could *see* the hole that was missing after he'd left."

"That's deep," Michael replied. He'd meant it honestly, but the words didn't come out that way.

"I'm just saying... Anyway, what about that date with, uh, don't tell me... Trina! How'd that go?"

Michael shrugged. "She was nice enough. I don't think it's going to work out."

Colton glanced at him in disbelief. "You could tell all that just from one date?"

"Yeah."

His boss scoffed. "I don't think I ever met someone I could write off that quickly. Definitely not a gal. You must've played Twenty Questions to get to know her that fast."

"Yeah."

His boss scoffed again, but thankfully dropped the subject. Instead, the old man went back to talking about the fish he'd caught and how he and his buddy had already planned their next weekend out.

Colton went on, "It was a little dreary, sure, but we got some parkas and made do. Sad I missed the weather here though. You guys had a beautiful weekend."

Michael nodded along, realizing that, in fact, they had nothing but sunshine both Saturday and Sunday.

At some point, Colton trailed off and turned up the oldies on the radio.

AFTER WORK, MICHAEL HEATED up leftovers and slunk down into his reclining chair. He felt exhausted, even though he'd just had one of the easiest days he could remember.

He chalked it up to the last few nights' sleep, or lack thereof.

Hopefully, tonight he would sleep better.

Michael was already reaching for the remote, about to put on a movie, when the chimney caught his eye.

The plastic container he'd put under the drip early this morning was half-full, which was disconcerting because it wasn't a small container. He stared and waited for nearly a minute before breathing a sigh of relief. At least it had stopped dripping.

Michael pushed himself up from his chair, went over and picked up the container.

He grimaced.

The water was dark, but had congealed so that the darker and thicker material floated to the surface. There were clumps of stringy material that Michael could only guess were strands of insulation. Chunks of dark red speckled the mass…

The wrapper of the insulation. Had to be. Something must have made a nest in there at one point and chewed up a bunch of the insulation.

But none of that helped him stomach the smell. It smelled rotten, and he had the brief vision of a dead squirrel twisted up in the insulation and rotting in the chimney.

Goddamn, Michael hoped he was wrong.

Carefully, he walked the container to the back door, then out to the back of the yard, and dumped it along the fence line. Then he rinsed it out as best he could with the hose. It looked like the shit had stained the plastic, but Michael didn't feel like washing it with soap and water. Instead, he took it back inside and placed it under the chimney again.

Then he plopped down in his chair and turned on the TV.

He scrolled for something to watch, but his mind drifted to his sister, Ellie. He tried to think back to the last time he'd hung out with her and Darryl—the last time they'd went out for dinner or even just had a night in together… He couldn't remember.

He should call or even just send a text. Just something to say that they *should* get together soon. Not just when they're cleaning out their dead parents' house.

But as Michael settled back in his chair, the thought faded. Another day, when he wasn't so damn tired.

Besides, Ellie would probably tell him to get a girlfriend. God knew they saw each other much less once she'd met Darryl—not that she and Michael had seen each other much before then.

The girl from his dreams wouldn't be so bad if it wasn't for that tongue thing. Michael chuckled—Hell, he even liked that fact that she didn't talk. That was probably why he felt so at ease in his dreams, at least in the beginnings of them: He didn't have to worry about what to say or how to keep a conversation going, or worry about when he was talking too much or too little or about something his date wasn't interested in.

Michael pushed the thought from his head and settled into watching TV. Maybe he'd find a new show to binge.

CHAPTER 6

At some point, Michael fell asleep in his chair with the TV playing.

In his dream, he was driving home. Bringing Her home.

She was looking eagerly out the passenger window as they drove through the neighborhood. Every now and then, Michael would catch her leg jittering with excitement, but he couldn't see her face. She was too busy looking out the window. All he saw was the back of her dark hair and her out of the corner of his eye.

Michael cleared his throat, but she didn't turn.

"You know, I still don't know your name..." he said absently.

But she just jittered with excitement.

Michael knew that she wasn't going to tell him.

He pulled into the driveway, and she opened the car door and practically sprinted to his front door. She waited for him expectantly, staring through the long dark hair that covered half her face.

She looked beautiful, if a little disheveled. In the sun, he saw stains on her dress—ones he hadn't noticed before. And her hair was a little ragged, like she'd gotten out of the shower and hadn't brushed it.

Again, Michael felt that pit of fear in his stomach—the one he felt the last time he'd brought a woman home. God, even the last time he'd been on a date.

Michael forced himself to walk to the front door. Forced himself to open it and invite her in. He wanted to. Maybe he needed to.

The dream skipped and a moment later, he was sitting in his recliner and she was sitting on the arm of it, pale legs dangling over the edge.

Michael rambled on, talking about his life, his neighbor, his job, and his boss. About anything and everything.

Meanwhile, she was listening intently from behind her curtain of dark hair. Listening and running her fingers lightly over his forearm.

He talked about how he wasn't satisfied with life. How he was depressed and that it wasn't the first time he'd felt that way. He went on about needing something else, but he was never quite sure what would scratch that itch or fill the void. Anything to make the emptiness go away or numb it.

Michael talked so long he almost forgot she was there.

In the dream, he had reclined back in the chair and tried to pull her close. He wanted nothing more than to feel her skin on his, to play with her hair, to kiss her. He wanted so much more, but he couldn't think past those innocent first steps.

Instead of cuddling into his arms, the girl left.

Michael's arm trailed out after her and wordlessly he wished she would come back.

She walked over to the chimney and crawled up inside it.

TUESDAY WAS A LONG install day, which was fine by Michael.

There were half a dozen guys on the job that day installing a heat pump in the attic and down in the unfinished basement. Michael and Colton got there earlier than the HVAC team so they could run some of the preliminary wiring; that way, the two teams could work around each other and not be in each other's way.

Michael knew most of the team, but having something to do kept people from talking to him; he wasn't in the mood. Michael gave a cursory greeting but otherwise kept to himself. He hadn't slept worth a shit last night either.

Maybe it was the dreaming. He had an old flame once that said that dreams kept her from getting a good night's sleep. It didn't matter if they were scary, short, or long—any kind of dream kept her from feeling rested when she woke up.

Up until last week, Michael hadn't remembered most of his dreams. He'd wake up with vague recollections or the memory of a single moment—like a snapshot. Most of the time, he didn't dream. Maybe it was being on his phone too much or watching TV before going to bed. Either way, the past few days were out of the ordinary.

Michael climbed the pull-down stairs to the attic, the rungs creaking beneath his weight. He carried three spools of wires over his shoulder and his tool belt bumped against the hatch as he stepped into the attic—short and squat.

It was a warm day and the attic was stifling already. Somehow he always managed to pick wrong. He'd try to get out of a hot attic and wind up in a cricket covered crawlspace. Or he'd pick the basement, only to find it unfinished and littered with spiders. Or Michael would think he'd lucked out when working on a ground-floor level unit and the internal wiring would be shot.

Michael tried the pull chain for the attic light, but the bulb was dead. He muttered a curse—he'd forgotten his helmet light in the truck. So Michael pulled out his flashlight and turned it on.

From there he traversed the beams, stepping carefully, watching both his footing and his head. The last thing he needed was to step on flimsy plywood and put his leg through the ceiling.

Michael stepped from beam to beam across the attic to where Colton had drilled pilot holes. His flashlight caught on shredded bits of insulation, old panes of glass, and bars that might've been from a bed frame or coat rack.

But his eyes lingered on the shredded bits of insulation. It was the same pinkish red as what was stuffed up in his chimney at home, except that this was in far better condition. Only the paper backing was tan—not red.

Maybe his eyes had played tricks on him the other night...

Or maybe the red chunks he'd found dripping into that container were from whatever squirrel or rat had made a home in his chimney—not from the insulation.

Michael shuddered and turned back to the task at hand.

He'd deal with the chimney when he got to it, so long as whatever animal might be up here in the attic with him knew enough to piss off and leave him alone.

He had no desire to have a repeat of that crawl space from the other day and come face to face with another rat.

TUESDAY NIGHT, MICHAEL DREAMED again.

He was sitting in his reclining chair. She was sitting on the arm again and running her fingers over his forearm.

"It sucks," Michael said as he rambled. "It just all blurs together. One job to another. One drive to another."

He snuck a glance at Her. She was smiling from behind her dark hair. A coy, maybe even flirtatious, smile. One that made Michael nervous.

He continued rambling. "It just doesn't feel worth it, you know? To keep doing what I'm doing. I don't really know what I'm doing.

"I used to tell myself that everyone else felt the same way—that we were all just making shit up as we went, that no one really knew what they were doing either.

"But that's bullshit. My parents knew what they were doing. Colton does. Ellie and Darryl know what they're doing.

"I'm just tired of pretending. I can't do it anymore. I just don't know what else to do, or what I need..."

Michael wanted to look at her, but couldn't bring himself to meet her eyes. He wanted her—in that moment, he wanted her more than anything. But that old terror was still there, burning a hole in his stomach like he'd drank battery acid.

"Maybe Colton was right. Maybe I just need someone... even if it's just for the night. Just someone to take my mind—Ow!"

Michael jerked his arm away from Her. His forearm oozing blood from four long gashes—where she'd dug her nails into him. He winced and clutched his arm to stop the bleeding.

"What did you do that—"

Michael looked at Her and he froze.

Through the thin openings in her hair, Michael finally saw her face. The skin of her face was stretched tight around her eyes and cheeks. Her eyes were white and glazed over. Her mouth...

Her mouth hung open, jaw slack, but it was too long. Her cheeks were stretching like melting candle wax or gum, and her mouth was a black void where teeth or a tongue should've been.

Michael stared—both captivated and horrified—at the twisted face that was only a foot away from his own.

A face that was leaning toward him, her mouth yawning wider. She gripped the cushions of the chair tight and the fabric tore in her grasp.

Michael pushed back as far as he could, the chair finally reaching the end of its extension. She only leaned closer until her face was inches from his and from deep inside the pit of her mouth, a tongue writhed and extended toward him.

Michael woke from his dream, yanking his hands up toward him so quickly he nearly hit himself in the face. He sat up and when he realized he was no longer sleeping, Michael grabbed his phone.

2:35 AM

Michael sighed, too scared from his dream to be frustrated. He set his phone down and rubbed his eyes.

Light from the moon bled through the curtains, casting the living room in an eerie glow.

Out of the corner of his eye, by the chimney, Michael swore he saw something move.

Saw something slither back up the chimney.

CHAPTER 7

MICHAEL NEARLY TOOK OFF Wednesday.

How many days had it been since he got a good night's sleep?

It didn't matter how long he slept, he was ungodly tired when the alarm came at four in the morning.

And his creepy-ass dreams weren't helping.

Michael made coffee and got ready for work. As he did, he scrolled through his phone and stopped at Jessica Chambers.

He stared at her number, coffee pot in hand.

His old friend—and friend with benefits—was still in there. Whether she had the same number remained to be seen.

The coffee pot trembled in his hand.

Maybe it was the fact that he was sleep deprived, but for a long moment, he wasn't sure why he'd scrolled to Jessica's number. They'd had some fun together, but that wasn't all of it. In between their romps, she'd also been one of the only women he'd really talked to and confided in.

He missed that, and he needed that right now.

Hell, Jessica had also been interested in dreams and theories about them. Maybe she could help him figure out what was going on in his head.

Michael finished pouring his coffee and stared at the phone on the counter.

That was all if she didn't have a boyfriend. She had a habit of going dark when she was in a relationship. She might very well block Michael's texts.

Could he blame her though? He wouldn't want an old flame texting him out of the blue and getting him in trouble with his girlfriend.

Michael groaned and took a long sip of coffee—promptly burning the ever-loving shit out of his mouth and tongue. He cursed and got a glass of tap water to sip on.

Then he groaned and typed out a message to Jessica, making sure to schedule it for a more bearable hour of the morning.

Michael 9:20 AM: *Hey* (Scheduled)

Then he only had a few hours to wait.

Michael was riding with his boss to the second job of the day when he got a text back from Jessica. His hands clammed up as he unlocked his phone.

Jessica 9:24 AM: *Hey yourself*

Colton reached over and slapped his shoulder. "What're you smirking at?"

"Nothing," Michael muttered back.

"Yeah, I bet it's *nothing*," Colton replied. Michael could hear the smirk in his boss's voice without looking at him.

Michael 9:26 AM: *Wasn't sure if you would reply*

Jessica 9:27 AM: *You caught me at a good time*

Michael 9:28 AM: *In the morning?*

Jessica 9:28 AM: *Between boyfriends*

Michael 9:30 AM: *We should get together*

Jessica 9:31 AM: *What did you have in mind?*

Michael 9:32 AM: *Maybe dinner. My place. Tonight?*

Jessica 9:37 AM: *Yes. Make spaghetti. I'll bring wine*

Michael closed his phone and sighed. He already felt nervous, but at least he hadn't chickened out.

"So, is it Trina?"

Michael shook his head. "Nah, an old girl." When Colton glanced sidelong at him, he added, "Jessica."

"Oh, Jessica."

"You don't remember Jessica."

Colton scoffed. "She's about the only name that kept coming up. She's still single?"

Michael nodded.

"Well, there you go. Have yourself some fun and get yourself out of this damn rut you're in."

Michael nodded again and then closed his eyes.

Colton let Michael off early so he could go grocery shopping and clean house.

Jessica 3:19 PM: *Is it okay if I come over 5?*

Michael 3:22 PM: *Yeah sure*

By the time she came over, Michael had picked up and cleaned up most of the house—most of the things he hadn't gotten to before cleaning for Trina.

When he was done cleaning, Michael showered, shaved, and trimmed up. Then he threw on some old cologne that he knew that she liked—probably the same almost empty bottle that he'd had since the last time she came around.

Then he turned on the TV and waited, resisting the urge to crack open a beer.

Five o'clock came and went, and at 5:15, there was a knock at the door.

Michael opened it to find Jessica smiling at him, and holding up a bottle of Vince red.

She looked like she'd stepped right out of his memories. Her light blond hair was still cropped and she still wore that same purple lipstick. She'd worn an oversized hoodie and shorts.

Michael looked her up and down, tried to whistle, and failed. He'd always loved her legs.

"Yeah, yeah," Jessica said, smirking. "Are you going to invite me in?"

He did and shut the door behind her.

Jessica kicked her shoes off, walked to the kitchen, and set the wine down on the table like she'd been over to visit yesterday.

Michael smiled and gestured to the door. "I didn't see your car outside."

"I got a lift. My car's been acting up."

"Still driving the Toyota?" Michael asked, walking past her to the stove.

Jessica smiled and nodded. "Yep."

They carried on while Michael started the water for the noodles. She asked about his work and about Colton. Jessica was still working as a receptionist at the dentist's office up the road. She just got out of a relationship.

She asked if he'd been seeing anyone recently, and Michael hesitated. He turned and stirred the noodles idly.

Jessica sidled up beside him at the stove and smirked. "So that's why you texted me."

"That's not the only reason," he joked.

"Why else?"

Her face seemed to hang somewhere between playful and serious, and Michael didn't know what to say. So he continued stirring the noodles. Maybe if he kept it up long enough, Jessica would forget about the question.

Instead, Jessica laid her head on his shoulder and stared at the pot too.

She'd done that before, probably the last time they got together.

Just feeling her put Michael—a little—at ease.

Michael let out a sigh he didn't know he'd been holding, and Jessica wrapped her arm around his. She'd always been good at that: Those little touches.

And it had been so long since he'd been touched.

He stared at the pot because he couldn't bring himself to look at her or kiss her. Because if he did, he might cry.

Instead, he stared at the pot of noodles, and the sauce warming beside it. Let the smell of tomato, onion, and basil fill his thoughts.

He'd probably made spaghetti for her the last time she came over, or last time he crashed at her place. How many times had he made it for her?

"Can I ask you something?"

Jessica chuckled, but didn't let go. "Yes, since you prefaced."

"Why didn't we work out?"

"You didn't want something serious."

She said it so plainly that it almost made him flinch. Michael somehow managed to stay still—caught between Jessica and a hot stove. Had he really been so callous? Had she really wanted to be with him—for more than a night? Had he fucking glossed over that fact?

The timer went off on the stove, pulling him out of his train of thoughts. Michael drained the noodles and added the sauce while Jessica set a table for two—still remembering where the plates and silverware were.

It didn't hit him until after he set the pot on the table between them, until after they'd started eating and after they'd started talking about old times.

It didn't hit Michael until Jessica had pulled him to the couch, until they were wrapped in each other's arms.

Three years. It had been three years since they'd talked. Did he really think things would be the same between them after that long? Did he hope they would?

That fact didn't help Michael relax as their hands explored one another. Jessica's fingers traced his neck and his chest, and Michael sighed. *She remembered*, and he repaid her in kind, running his fingers along her back just how she liked.

As she reached lower, Michael realized with muted horror just how nervous he was.

"You still like that, right?" Jessica asked, leaning close to his ear.

He nodded and told her earnestly that he was nervous.

Jessica licked his ear, then smirked. "Well, I know one thing that always works."

She slid off the couch and between his legs, then set to unbuckling his belt.

She was about to slide his pants off when the plastic container shook. Michael saw something move over by the chimney—something stringy.

Like something with long dark hair had been watching, and snuck back up inside the chimney before he could see it. Or her.

"Hey, let's, uh, take this to my room." Michael muttered, grabbing Jessica's hands.

She smiled. "Okay."

Chapter 8

That night Michael didn't dream, and it was wonderful.

After he'd confirmed with Jessica, Michael had asked his boss if he could come in late the next day. Colton had told him enthusiastically to take the day if "it would get him out of his funk."

Michael woke up in his bed and rolled over to look at his phone. Six o'clock. He promptly decided that he could sleep in a little longer.

He rolled back over to hold Jessica, maybe even wake her up for round three, but she wasn't there.

Michael wiped his eyes and patted the bed. Yep, she wasn't there.

Thinking she'd gotten up to go to the bathroom, Michael laid back down and waited.

And waited.

"Jessica?" he called out. When she didn't answer, he called out louder, "Jessica?"

He rolled over and sat on the edge of the bed. Jessica's clothes were gone, everything except her panties—which might've been hot in other circumstances.

Michael pulled on his pants and walked out of his bedroom. It was still dark outside, so he flipped on lights as he went. There was no light on in the bathroom...

Jessica wasn't there.

Dumbfounded, he walked the rest of the short way to the kitchen. There was no sign of her.

"What the Hell?" Michael muttered as he walked another lap of the house.

Michael pulled out his phone and texted her.

Michael 6:13 AM: *Hey where are you?*

Then he paced around the house while he waited for a response.

Michael 6:18 AM: *Did you go to work early?*

Michael 6:25 AM: *Are you okay?*

He put on a pot of coffee and slowly began to feel ridiculous.

Jessica was probably driving, or at work already. Either way, she probably couldn't respond.

Or maybe it was something he did...

Michael leaned on the counter, going back over the night as the coffee dripped. No, last night was fine. But

God, if he kept texting her like this, she'd probably think he'd lost it.

Instead, he texted Colton that he could meet him at the next job site. Michael didn't really feel like sitting around the house, waiting, worrying, or moping. Work would take his mind off of things.

Michael sipped on his coffee and got ready for work, all the while keeping an eye on his phone.

Jessica never texted him back that morning. Never called.

He put on the rest of his work clothes, grabbed his lunch, and then walked to the door.

Jessica's shoes were still by the door.

Michael stared at them, completely confused and beginning to worry.

He glanced back through the kitchen to the living room, wondering one last time if he'd overlooked her clothes lying around.

There was no other trace of Jessica.

MICHAEL WAS QUIET AT work. Colton asked a few questions, but must have seen the look on Michael's face.

Michael kept looking at his phone, waiting for a response.

It was hard to concentrate. He shocked himself good on a basement receptacle when he crossed the wrong wires.

He muttered a few curses, then tried harder to mind what he was doing.

By the time the work van pulled around to his house that morning, Michael still hadn't heard from Jessica.

He was sweating through clothes, and he hadn't spoken a word to Colton on the drive home. He was beyond worried. The entire day, his mind had raced, wondering where Jessica was or what might've happened to her.

Clearly, she'd left in a hurry—there wasn't any other explanation.

Maybe she'd gotten dressed in a hurry in the middle of the night, called a ride, and left.

That would explain her underwear. She'd just found her shorts and thrown them on in a hurry. *Shit*, but what about her shoes? How could she have run off in the middle of the night without her shoes? What could have possibly have happened that made her run off in the middle of the night and not paused to put on her shoes?

A jealous ex, maybe? That would explain why she wasn't texting back... Maybe she was in a bad relationship and hadn't told him.

That explanation definitely didn't make him feel any better.

None of it was good. There was no good reason why Jessica would've left—snuck out—in the middle of the night in a hurry and left her goddamn shoes.

Michael got out of the van, gave Colton a half-hearted wave, and walked away. He felt like he was going to pass out and had to remind himself to breathe.

Felipe was working in the yard and turned to greet him. Michael gave him a half-hearted wave too.

"Saw you had a lady friend over, my man... Did, uh, did it not go so well?"

He didn't respond.

Felipe stood up and stepped closer to the fence. "Hey, why don't you come over and have a few beers? We can talk about it—or not."

"Maybe another time, Felipe." Michael walked past his neighbor and into his house.

He just wanted to be alone.

He probably would have a few beers. Something to take his mind off of things.

Something to put him to sleep.

Anything to take his mind off of things.

MICHAEL TURNED ON THE TV because he couldn't stand the silence of the house. Then he cracked open a beer while he watched the same comfort shows he'd seen a dozen times.

It kept him from staring at the fireplace.

The plastic container was nearly full of dark liquid again. Michael didn't walk over closer to inspect it.

It didn't appear to be dripping at the moment, so he told himself it could wait until the morning. Until it was light outside again.

Drinking helped, and he drank until he felt drowsy enough to go to bed.

Through the evening, he kept pushing aside thoughts of something living in his chimney. Of the mold and mildew that was growing inside it.

And that the girl from his dreams was living up there.

It was a stupid thought, and Michael laughed at himself. Tried to anyway.

It didn't push aside the dread. The creeping feeling of something wrong with the chimney. Wrong with the house. With him.

At the very least, something had died up there.

For a moment, the twisted thought came that Jessica was up there, shoved between the stones and twisted on herself that her body would fit.

Michael flinched in his recliner, spilling beer down the front of his shirt. He chugged what was left and quickly got up to get another one from the fridge.

Careful not to look at the chimney on the way by or on the way back.

He brought three beers back and set them beside the chair. They were gone before the next movie ended

Then he turned off the TV, left the cans, and went to bed.

He didn't want to sleep in the living room.

MICHAEL WOKE TO SCRATCHING. Scratching and tapping.

At first, he thought it might've been raining outside. Sometimes when it was windy, the bush branches would scrape the small window in his room.

But it wasn't raining and there wasn't any wind.

The sounds were coming from behind his bedroom door.

Michael lay in bed, absolutely still.

Maybe it was the rat or bat or whatever poor bastard had made a nest in his chimney, finally fallen through and scurrying around on his floor.

He lay still and listened, because he wanted to be absolutely sure of what it was.

The sounds were coming from along the bottom of the door and along the floor. It almost sounded like the thing was pacing back and forth, looking for a gap to crawl through.

In the darkness of the room, Michael almost thought he could make out the shadow of something moving behind the door.

Something bigger than a rat.

Then the tapping and scratching sounds rose, like the animal was standing on its hind legs and feeling along the door.

Up and up.

Until the sounds were coming from around the doorknob.

No rat was that big.

The doorknob rattled.

Michael couldn't breathe. He stared at the shaking doorknob, wondering whether he'd locked the door to his room. Had he? Would he have? He'd been afraid when he'd gone to sleep, so maybe he had...

Something sharp scraped the metal knob, making a scratch and a short screech. The knob jiggled but didn't turn.

He had locked it.

Michael breathed out as quietly as he could, still refusing to move beneath the covers.

He was dreaming. He had to be.

Michael slowly pulled the covers up to his chin and closed his eyes. Please be dreaming. Please... Please...

CHAPTER 9

THE NEXT MORNING SUCKED. Michael woke in a cold sweat, his clothes and sheets soaked through. He was freezing. He felt disgusting.

And hungover.

His head throbbed as he rolled over and turned off the alarm on his phone.

Then he rolled and stared at his bedroom door. It was closed, and the house was quiet.

Had last night just been a bad dream?

It had been, Michael decided all too quickly. Anything else was ridiculous.

It must've been raining. Must have been the bush beside his window making all that racket.

He really should cut back on his drinking.

At least it was Friday.

He stood, clutching his head, and stumbled toward the bedroom door. He stood for a long moment, waiting and listening.

When he was absolutely sure that nothing was out there, he unlocked and opened the door.

His living room was just as he left it. Michael wasn't sure what he'd been preparing himself to find, but the furniture was all fine and the floor wasn't dirty. He'd just vacuumed the other day. A blanket or two were out of place, but they'd been that way since Jessica had been over.

Jessica...

Michael checked his phone. Still nothing from Jessica.

He wasn't worried anymore. He was past that. What was past being worried about someone? Michael just felt numb, like whatever bad thing had already happened and he was just waiting around to get the horrible news.

That's how it had been when Dad passed. They all knew he'd had a heart attack... It just took two hours for the doctors to confirm it. Those two hours had been like sitting in a box of glass, watching the world go by, but everything around feeling muted.

That was how Michael felt now, like he was a puppet being pulled along, deaf and numb to what was going on. Just going through the motions until the news finally reached him and cut his strings and he fell to the ground in a heap.

Coffee didn't help his headache.

Usually, Colton ragged on him when he was hungover, but today his boss was silent. Didn't even ask Michael if he wanted to talk.

That was fine by Michael. How the Hell could he explain what had happened anyway?

Yeah, my fuck buddy up and disappeared. Left her shoes and everything.

I think her secret abusive boyfriend kidnapped her.

I think she got eaten. No, not by the boyfriend.

Michael rubbed his temples and turned the air vent so the AC was blowing on his face. It was going to be a long day.

And he wasn't even looking forward to being done with work or looking forward to going back to sleep in his bed, or being home all weekend.

Michael wasn't sure he wanted to go back home at all.

COLTON TRIED MAKING SMALL talk during their middle check of the day. They were outside an old Victorian house, leaning over to look at the outside unit.

Colton prattled on about how nice of a night it was. How he'd slept with the windows open for the first time in weeks. He'd managed to position the fan just right so that it kept a nice breeze going all night.

Michael didn't say anything.

Even though he was outside, kneeling next to Colton, his mind flashed back to the night before—

Laying in bed, listening to scratching and scraping.

"It didn't rain last night?" Michael asked absently.

Colton's head was buried inside the panel of the unit and he paused for a moment, surprised at Michael's reply. "Not a lick," Colton finally said.

Michael's heart pounded. He stood up and laced his fingers behind his head, focusing on the sun beating down on his face.

He wasn't back in his room. It was the middle of the day. He was standing in the middle of a customer's backyard, his boots crunching on dry grass.

He wasn't back in his room, listening to scratching and scraping on the other side of his bedroom door.

He was safe.

"ARE YOU SURE YOU'RE alright?" Colton asked as they pulled up in front of Michael's house.

Michael grunted.

"Well, if you need a few days off. Just take them—after the weekend, I mean."

"No work tomorrow?" Michael asked.

"Not tomorrow. Even if I had something... You need to take some time. Get yourself straight or get yourself some sleep. Get *something*, just fix yourself."

Michael nodded along, not listening.

No work tomorrow meant he was going to be in his house for the next two days.

He stared out the window at the front door.

It looked harmless enough. It certainly didn't look like anything was wrong. Even the chimney peeking over the roof looked perfectly fine from the driveway.

So why did Michael have such a bad feeling...

"Hey—"

Michael startled and turned toward Colton.

"I was just saying, give me a ring if you want to talk, or if you need some help around the house." Colton gestured to the lawn.

"Yeah," Michael muttered in reply. Then he got out and waved over his shoulder.

Michael walked with hands clenched. He glanced at the grass on the way to the front door.

It did look long. Maybe he could take care of the yard tomorrow morning.

If he could sleep through the night.

Michael stood at the front door, keys in hand, frozen. He stared at the doorknob, imagining that he heard something scratching behind the door—waiting for the knob to jiggle.

Or waiting for the door to swing open, for the girl of his dreams to be standing in front of him.

That she would grab his wrist and drag him into the house and slam the door behind them, or pull him into an embrace and snake her long tongue into his mouth and down his throat.

Michael shuddered.

On the street, the work van backfired as Colton turned around and drove off.

Michael stood there, breathing hard, keys shaking in his hands.

He dropped his work bag on the porch, turned, and walked to his car.

Then he drove to the liquor store.

If he was going to stay in his house, he sure as fuck wasn't going to stay sober.

THAT NIGHT, MICHAEL STUMBLED through his house. He'd lost track of how many beers he drank, and trying to count them was far too difficult. Cans had piled up in the corner of his chair and across the floor.

He had gotten up to go to the kitchen to get another drink, and he'd nearly made it.

Michael slumped against the wall of the kitchen, propped up on his shoulder.

He'd overdone it.

He couldn't remember the last time he'd gotten so drunk he had trouble standing and walking. Michael had managed to turn the light on in the kitchen, but he slowly slumped down until he was kneeling on the ground.

Shit. He was about to throw up.

It was only with concentrated effort and drunken force of will that he didn't.

Minutes passed there on the floor.

Then came the sound of dripping.

Michael turned to the kitchen window, wondering if it was raining, but he didn't see anything outside. No raindrops against the window.

The dripping was coming from the chimney. Michael thought he heard the crinkle of paper—of insulation.

He turned, rolling over, and stumbling to his feet and out to the living room. He slumped against the wall. Across the living room, black water was dripping into the plastic bucket under the chimney.

Drip. Drip. Drip.

Michel watched, spellbound and unable to move as the dripping grew faster, until they were beating in time with his heart.

Drip drip. Drip. Drip drip drip.

Long, thin points stretched down from the chimney, like rat's tails or the legs of a massive bug, but they were a sickly pale color.

Four of them. Then a fifth. Each over a foot long.

It wasn't until they wrapped around the chimney that Michael realized what they really were.

Breath caught in his throat. He was pushing back against the wall now, trying to scoot backward into the kitchen—anywhere away from the chimney—but he was too afraid to turn away.

They were fingers. The fingers wrapped around the edge of the chimney, gripping the bricks tight, like something was pulling itself down through. Through the insulation that was stuffed up and should've been blocking the way.

Drip drip, drip drip. Splash. Drip. Splash. Drip drip.

Chunks of bright red were falling into the bowl, large enough to be visible from across the room. They splashed murky black water across the stones. Onto the surrounding carpet.

All this time, Michael had been telling himself that they were chunks of insulation, but they were too heavy. The splashes were too much to be something as light as insulation.

The red chunks were bright, and so slick they shined in the dim light from the kitchen.

Strands of black came down next, the tips falling into the plastic container.

Matted black hair.

Michael's eyes were wide. He couldn't breathe.

A pale forehead emerged from the chimney and two milky-white eyes peeked out from behind the brick.

He stared at Her. She stared at him, neither moving.

Then her fingers flexed, and the girl from his dreams crawled downward like a spider—

And as the rest of her smiling face came into view, Michael gasped and sat up in bed.

His breath was ragged, but he's breathing. He was in bed, not slumped against the kitchen wall. Not staring at the chimney.

The room was dark, but not so dark that Michael couldn't see the door to his bedroom.

It was open.

Michael lunged forward, kicking off his sweat-soaked sheets, stumbling still-drunk toward the door. He tripped and caught himself. Made it to the door and slammed it shut. Locked it.

He fell to the ground and slid backward until he was at the foot of the bed. He stared at the door, waiting.

As the silence dragged on, Michael's breath slowed and he started to sob.

Chapter 10

Michael woke up on the floor by the foot of his bed. He'd fallen back asleep.

He crawled over to his phone, which read 10:39 AM.

Had he really slept through the night?

No—he'd woken up on the floor. Last night... That had happened. It hadn't been a dream.

Michael stared at the door... Maybe it had been a hallucination, like sleep paralysis. He'd been really drunk. That had to be it. Sleep paralysis.

He crawled back over to the entrance and put his face to the floor to try to peer under the door. It was no use; there wasn't enough space between the door and the carpet.

Michael stood up, then promptly sat back down on the edge of his bed. He was *still* really drunk.

Slowly and methodically, he pulled on a new pair of pants and a shirt, and then readied himself to open the door. It was a longer process than he would admit.

And his hand trembled as he turned the lock and as he turned the doorknob. His breath was ragged as he opened the door.

The living room was just as he'd left it. A little disheveled—he'd never put away the blankets or picked up his beer cans—but other than that... it was empty.

Timidly, he looked at the fireplace.

The plastic container was full of black water, and it had spilled over the top, covering the fireplace in a wet, black sheen. Chunks of red lay in the dried puddle, sticking out like morbid shells on a beach.

Michael couldn't bring himself to walk over to the chimney, so he walked around the edge of the room to the windows and opened them one by one. As if light would help keep whatever he was afraid of at bay.

Nothing happened as light flooded the room. Michael wasn't sure what he expected, but he was a little relieved.

He shuffled back the way he came, along the edge of the room, until he got to the kitchen. Then he made coffee and poured cereal, all while keeping his eyes on the chimney.

Yard work. That's what he needed to do today.

Anything other than stay in the goddamn house.

"Hey, my man!"

Michael looked over and found Felipe leaning on the fence. He killed the lawnmower and pulled off his ear protection.

"Hey, Michael, how are you doing?"

Michael smirked. He had to look as bad as he felt—like shit. "I've been better."

Felipe smiled awkwardly. "I wasn't going to say nothing, but hey, it can't be that bad. Saw you had a girl over the other night."

"Are you keeping tabs on me, Felipe?"

"Naw, naw. My wife, she happened to see. It was a good thing, right?"

Michael nodded. "I thought it was, but I haven't heard from her. I think... I think it was a one time thing."

"Hey, sometimes those are good, too."

Michael wasn't sure what else to say, and silence settled between the two men.

"Look," Felipe said, "How about you come over tonight? Unless you got other plans?" Michael shook his head, and Felipe added, "Then I insist. We got some beer. Tequila too, if you can stomach it. My wife said you can even crash on the floor if you want. Okay, she didn't say that part, but if you need to, then you need to. I know not all of you gringos can handle your tequila."

Michael looked back at his house. His head was pounding and he felt like he was sweating beer. Any other time in his life, he would've turned Felipe down, but now... He'd briefly thought about sleeping outside tonight instead of in his house.

Michael forced a smile. "Just make sure there's enough tequila for the both of us."

By the time Michael finished yardwork, it was a little after noon. Felipe hadn't said anything about dinner or about when to come over, but Michael figured he'd meant *this evening*.

So Michael waited.

Besides, if he went over now, he and Felipe might start early and end early... If they started drinking later, maybe Felipe would let him crash on the floor; that way he didn't have to come home.

Michael stood just off of his porch, staring at his own front door. Afraid to go inside his own home.

He should at least freshen up and change his clothes. Felipe's wife (Michael had forgotten her name) was already being nice enough to host him. The least he could do was show up *not* looking like a bum.

Michael forced himself to go inside. He crept through the kitchen, around the edge of his living room, and into the bedroom. He shut the door and locked it, then proceeded to grab a change of clothes and a stick of deodorant.

Then he mustered up the courage to go back to the kitchen.

Breathing quickly, he grabbed a dishrag and soaped it up to give himself a quick sponge bath, then wiped himself down with the nearby towel. He changed and left all the dirty clothes and rags on the floor, then turned to leave.

He stopped at the front door and looked back through the house.

It was still quiet. Still well-lit enough through the windows.

He stalked back through the house and turned on every light before grabbing the case of beer from the fridge and heading outside.

IT ACTUALLY WAS KIND of nice sitting out in his backyard. It wasn't much—only like an eighth of an acre—but it was nice and flat and the grass grew well enough. It was empty save for an old metal fire pit, but it was just what Michael needed.

He sat out back, dozing off in the grass.

Between that and the beers, it was almost enough to take his mind off of things.

Almost.

His mind drifted back to his grandma's engagement ring sitting in his dresser. All of this trouble—all the dreams—started after he brought home that ring. Maybe there was something there. Maybe a spirit had latched onto it or something, only that the woman didn't resemble his mom, his grandma, or any other woman in his family...

Finally, the thought left him. It wasn't like he was going to go back in the house to get the ring now.

It was almost six o'clock when Felipe called over the fence for him to come over. Michael brought the rest of his beer.

"You think we'll need all that?" Felipe asked.

Michael shrugged.

Felipe ushered him inside, and for the first time, Michael saw the inside of a neighbor's house.

Felipe's house was littered with knick knacks and toys. Michael had almost forgotten that they had kids. Toy trucks and tiny cars were so numerous that he had to watch his step through the entryway. The shelves and tables were almost as filled with porcelain strawberries and other fake fruit.

"Soon she'll put out the pumpkins," Felipe said, gesturing to the table. "Maria likes decorating for the seasons."

Maria, Michael said again in his head, trying to commit the name to memory. Felipe had to have told him her name before, but Michael had forgotten it.

Felipe ushered him through the house and turned a corner at the living room. Maria and three boys were sitting on the floor and watching a show on their TV.

Michael almost jumped when he saw Maria's long, dark hair.

"Maria, me and Michael are going to go down to the basement and have a little bro time."

One of the boys turned and waved. Maria smiled and waved them off. "I'll make you a snack later if you want it. Nice meeting you finally, Michael."

Michael stammered out a thank you. He was too busy trying to conceal his shock.

He followed Felipe around the corner and into the basement.

Felipe's basement was finished—dry walled and trimmed, but not painted.

"We never could decide on a color," Felipe said as he took Michael around.

It was small and cozy, in a sense. The kid's toys were stacked in an old playpen. A half-empty bookshelf sat next to it.

Two old couches sat in front of an old flatscreen TV. Felipe slid the mini-fridge closer until the cord was stretched taut; he could just reach the beers from the edge of the couch.

"It's not much, but it's something," Felipe said, handing him a beer.

Michael sat on the second couch. It sat at an angle so he could see both his host and the TV.

He took a drink and tried to put into words exactly what he was feeling.

"No, it's nice. It's really nice." Michael meant it in every sense of the word.

Felipe's drywall work was straight and smooth. Despite having two kids, the place was tidy. The couch he was sitting on was comfortably broken in. His beer was cold, and he couldn't imagine spending the evening drinking with many other people besides Felipe.

He felt safe here.

And self-conscious, like he was intruding on so much normalcy. Michael hoped that he looked more put together than he felt. He probably didn't.

They talked for a while. Felipe was good at that. He went on about work, the yard, Maria and the kids. Michael half-listened, but asked questions to keep him talking. Felipe seemed all too eager to fill the silence.

At some point, they started talking about movies to watch, when Michael got a message on his phone.

Unknown 6:38 PM: *Is this Michael?*

Michael 6:39 PM: *Yes. Who is this?*

Unknown 6:39 PM: *This is Connie. Jess's friend. Have you heard from Jess?*

Michael 6:42 PM: *No*

Michael's phone started ringing, and he excused himself and went around to the other side of the basement stairs.

"Hi, Michael. What do you mean you haven't heard from her?"

Michael swallowed and forced himself to breathe. Then he quietly told Connie about how he'd woken up to find Jessica gone, and that he'd texted her and she'd never replied. He left out the part about leaving her shoes in his house though.

Michael asked, "Did she have a boyfriend, or was she seeing someone else?"

"No... I, uh..."

"We were just friends... It wasn't serious. You can tell me."

"It's not that. I'm worried. Jess and I have been friends for a while, and she can be flighty, you know? Get wrapped up in a new guy sometimes, that kind of thing. But not like this. This isn't like her."

Michael swallowed nervously. "So, what do we do?"

"I'm going with her parents to the police to file a missing person's report."

"Okay."

"Are you okay?"

"Yeah... I don't know what to think."

Connie asked for Michael's information, and he gave it to her. The cops would want to speak to him, since Michael was the last person to see her or speak with her.

"I have to go. I have to call Jess's parents back. I guess we'll be in touch."

"Yeah. I have your number. Hey, let me know if you hear from her. Please."

"I will."

MICHAEL SAT BACK DOWN on the couch. He felt like he was going to pass out. After a moment, he reached over, grabbed his beer, and chugged the last half of it.

"So, Michael, what was that about?"

Michael sighed and told him exactly what he'd told Connie. Except that by the time Michael got to the part about her disappearing in the morning, he couldn't help thinking of Jessica pausing to look at the chimney on her way out, staring at matted dark hair and a long, bony hand reaching out.

"It will be okay," Felipe said, leaning over to get two more beers. "That's what the cops are for, right? She's missing and they find missing people. All you can do now is wait and not beat yourself up over it."

Michael listened, but he couldn't stop thinking of the woman in the chimney—her milky white eyes peering out from behind the bricks. Her neck twisting and body contorting as she crawled out of the chimney like a spider. Her mouth yawning open wider and wider into a black void—

Michael shuddered. "Yeah. Yeah. It will be okay." He turned to Felipe and before he could choose his words carefully, they just came out.

"Have you ever seen some strange shit?"

Felipe smirked, like he was trying to decide how serious Michael was being.

"Do you mean weird that can't be explained or that shouldn't be explained? Like Tijuana Dancing Cat weird, or ghosts you don't want to talk about weird?"

Michael said, "My mom passed away a while ago, and, uh, we were going through the rest of her stuff. Cleaning out the house. I brought some stuff home."

He thought back to his grandma's ring, and how all of this started with that.

"I think the ring might be haunted," Michael finally said. Then he told Felipe quickly about the apparition he'd been seeing.

Felipe stared at him, eyes narrowing, trying to figure out if he was full of bullshit.

After a long moment, Felipe said, "I've seen a lot of stuff…" He scoffed. "I'm not very religious anymore. The world's too random for it to be anything else. Sometimes good things happen for no reason. And sometimes, horrible, horrible shit finds us for the same reason. Which is to say, no reason at all. And sometimes that horrible thing just doesn't let go. Maybe the ring is that."

Michael suppressed a chill and shook his head in denial. "What am I supposed to do with that?"

"Get rid of the ring. See if it helps."

Michael stared at the coffee table.

Tomorrow. He'd get rid of the ring tomorrow. Fuck it.

CHAPTER 11

FELIPE BROKE OUT THE tequila a little while later, and a little while after that the night turned into a blur. At some point Felipe insisted they watch Telemundo, but that was all Michael remembered.

Michael woke up on the couch, head pounding like it was caught in a vice.

When he finally opened his eyes, Michael started to panic because he didn't remember where he was. It was a long, breathless moment before he remembered where he was.

Still in Felipe's basement.

He sighed with relief—so much he could've cried. Michael didn't dream last night, but he'd woken up in sweat-soaked clothes all the same.

Felipe was asleep on the other couch, snoring quietly.

Michael laid there, staring up at the ceiling. He knew what he had to do: He had to get rid of the ring. But he was terrified.

Because that meant he had to go back inside his house.

Michael fell back asleep and woke up around ten in the morning. Felipe was up and taking care of the small war-zone of empty cans.

"Not a bad night, my man," Felipe said, visibly wincing as cans clanked against one another in the trash bag. "No yard work for me today."

"Me neither," Michael muttered.

He helped Felipe pick up, then he hugged his neighbor goodbye.

If Felipe was surprised by it, he didn't say anything.

Michael went out the basement door and back to his house.

Michael stood at his own front door, key in hand, inches from the lock.

He could see through some of the shades that the lights were still on—just as he'd left them last night.

At least he wasn't living in some cliché horror movie where the lights flickered or suddenly went out.

No. That would be too predictable. He was living in a goddamn nightmare.

Finally, Michael held his breath, jammed the key into the lock, and opened the door.

The door creaked open, revealing an empty house. Everything was just how he left it: Dishes still in the sink, mail sitting on the table. Past the kitchen, he could see that blankets were still on the living room floor.

He stood in the doorway, absolutely still, and afraid to breathe. Just listening. Waiting.

Slowly, he stepped inside. Then waited again.

Michael only heard his own heart beating in his throat.

Another step. The floorboard creaked beneath him and Michael winced like he'd been shot.

He stayed as still as he could, waiting.

And when Michael still didn't hear anything, he walked slowly and steadily across the kitchen, and stopped in the doorway to the living room.

Michael shook his head in disbelief. The room looked exactly how he left it—

Except for the chimney.

The container he'd left there had overfilled and black water had run over the bricks and onto the carpet. A puddle of black pooled around the chimney, and even from across the room, Michael could see that it was still wet. Chunks of dark red glistened in the puddle.

Then the smell hit him—a wave of dank mold and mildew. The air felt thick with it.

It snapped him out of his trance, and Michael walked quickly around the corner to his bedroom. It too was just how he left it, sheets and blanket flung off the bed.

He walked to the dresser, opened the top drawer, and grabbed the ring. Then Michael turned to leave.

Drip.

Michael froze, the ring clenched in his hand.

Drip drip.

As quickly and quietly as he could, he walked to the door.

Black water was coming down the chimney in a steady drip.

Michael shuffled out of his room, his breath coming in ragged gasps.

Drip, drip. Drip.

He kept his back to the wall and his eyes on the chimney. HIs whole body was clenched, and when he finally got to the door to the kitchen, Michael turned and ran—

Knocking over a kitchen chair and nearly tripping—nearly dropping the ring.

The chair clanged on the tile and slid into the cabinet, but Michael was already grabbing his keys and running outside. He slammed the door behind him and locked it.

Michael leaned over, hands on his knees, trying to catch his breath.

But he didn't stay long. He turned and went to his car.

Even after he shut the door and started the engine—even as he was driving out of the neighborhood—Michael swore he could still hear dripping.

Michael drove until he was out of his neighborhood, then he pulled over on the side of the road. He looked up nearby pawn shops on his phone because he had no idea where he was going.

Apparently, there were five pawn shops nearby. He clicked the nearest one, *Big Lenny's,* and started driving.

Big Lenny's looked as sketchy as it sounded. It was a ragged building, sandwiched between three liquor stores.

Michael walked in, ignoring the taped-up signs advertising liquor next door and the tiny bell that rang as he entered. Inside smelled like cigarette smoke and mint air freshener.

He stepped inside and looked the place up and down. Glass cabinets lined the walls, haphazardly filled with jewelry—both men's and women's stacked together. Leather coats and fur coats hung on the right-side wall above the cabinets.

"Can I help you, son?" a man called from the back. He had a thick gray mustache, and his skin looked as worn as the coats on the walls.

Michael walked back, his eyes wandering to the rack of pistols and rifles behind the counter. Each had a tiny tag attached to it, but the writing was far too small to read.

"I have this ring." Michael set it on the counter.

The clerk picked up the ring. "May I?"

Michael grumbled before he realized the man wasn't really asking. He was already looking the ring over.

"Where'd you get it?"

"It was my grandma's. Mom passed and left it to me."

"You want to sell it or pawn it?"

"I, uh... sell it, I guess."

The clerk's mustache wrinkled and he set the ring back on the counter. "Two hundred."

Michael stared at the ring. It wasn't much, but it was worth a hell of a lot more than two hundred.

"That's it?"

The clerk shrugged. "You can try one of the other shops but they'll give you about the same. You can try online, but then you're waiting. You could sell it to a friend..."

Michael shook his head involuntarily. That was out of the question. For a moment, the thought crossed his mind that he should give Ellie the ring, but he'd put away the thought as quickly as it had come. She'd be pissed when she found out what Michael had done, but he just couldn't take the chance that the ring was the cause of all this.

God... could he really just pass this problem onto someone else? Someone he didn't know... How was that any better?

The clerk snapped his fingers. "Look, son, are you sure about this?"

Michael realized he'd been standing there for a long time. There were two other people behind him in line now. The man in the back of the line was grumbling.

Michael's stomach sank, and he felt like the words left his throat involuntarily.

"Yeah, I'm sure."

The clerk took the ring and slipped it beneath the glass. Then he opened his register and started counting bills.

Michael stared at his grandmother's ring through the glass. He just wanted to be rid of it.

He just wanted all of it to be over.

Chapter 12

MICHAEL WENT BACK HOME breathing just a little easier.

It felt like something had changed when he sold his grandmother's ring. Relief.

Of course, there was also some guilt for the poor bastard wound up with the ring next, but that guilt was a candle's warmth compared to being rid of the thing.

Michael pulled into his driveway, turned off the car, and sat there listening to the clicks and taps of the engine cooling down. It felt like a weight had been lifted off his shoulders, like he was finally moving past some horrible part of his life.

To think all he had to do was get rid of that stupid, tiny piece of jewelry. Who would've thought it would be that easy?

So, why was Michael still sitting in the car? Why couldn't he bring himself to get up and go inside?

Why was that sense of creeping dread still there? Like it was only silent because it was biding its time and waiting for Michael to lower his guard.

Lurking in the shadows, or in this case, in his chimney.

It was almost an hour later that Michael finally got out of the car and walked up to the door, fists clenched and shaking his head at himself.

He opened the door to find all the lights on, just as he'd left them, and the house utterly silent.

Michael crept inside and shut the door as quietly as he could, nearly gagging on the smell of mildew. He crept through the kitchen and peered at the chimney. It too was just how he'd left it: The plastic container filled to the top with black water. The surrounding bricks and carpet around the chimney were all soaked.

But the water was still. The chimney wasn't dripping.

That moment, Michael knew how he was spending the rest of his Sunday.

He turned back to the kitchen and began grabbing food—granola bars, peanut butter, crackers. All things that would keep at room temperature and were filling enough to get him through the evening. He grabbed a bottle of water and a bottle of rum, took everything to his bedroom, and dumped it all on the floor.

Then Michael locked himself in his room.

FOR THE REST OF the evening, Michael watched movies and scrolled the internet mindlessly on his phone. If he could make it to the end of the evening with his sanity, then he could take something to help him fall asleep or polish off the rest of the rum.

He'd be alright if he could just get some sleep and go to work tomorrow—if everything could just go back to normal.

When he had to piss, he climbed out through his tiny bedroom window and into the backyard. It wasn't the easiest thing to squeeze his ass through the opening, but he pushed over an end table and managed to do it without knocking anything over.

Throughout the evening he wore headphones, but kept the volume low so he could hear anything in the living room. But thankfully, the hours dragged on, boring and uneventful.

Until ten o'clock.

It was a few minutes past when Michael was about to take a sleeping pill. He planned on going to work tomorrow.

But then Michael thought he heard something from out in the living room. A trickle of water—

Followed by scurrying footsteps.

Michael dropped his bottle of water and the pill bottle.

The footsteps scurried all the way to the bedroom door and then stopped abruptly.

Michael's hands were shaking and his eyes were glued to the door.

Scratching came next. Instead of coming from one spot behind the door, it seemed to be spread out across the surface—like four long fingers were scratching in unison.

Michael quietly picked up the spare chair that sat at his computer desk and stepped close to the door. He tried to wedge it under the doorknob quietly, but when the knob jiggled, the scratching behind the door intensified.

Then it went for the doorknob, twisting it even though it was locked.

Michael backed away and fumbled for his closet door, opened it and grabbed the lone shoebox from the top shelf.

Inside was his dad's old revolver and a couple dozen rounds. It was already loaded, but Michael shakily opened the cylinder to double check. He left the shoebox of ammo on the top shelf.

Then he slumped down at the foot of his bed with his legs bracing the feet of the chair.

"Get the fuck out!" he shouted.

Tears streamed down his face and he clenched the revolver until his knuckles were white. No matter how hard he squeezed, his hands kept trembling.

The scratching subsided, then stopped completely.

Michael head footsteps leading away. Then the slosh of water as the container was tipped over.

Though he couldn't hear it, he imagined the woman crawled back up into the chimney.

MICHAEL WOKE ON THE living room couch. He was half-covered in blankets, one pulled up, nearly covering his entire face.

The shock and confusion of being in another room was quickly pushed aside—

His entire body felt heavy. He'd once read about the gravity on other planets being ten times or even hundreds of times Earth's gravity—that was how Michael felt now. It felt like he couldn't breathe. He was barely able to move at all, but somehow he peaked out from behind the blankets.

Something scurried behind the back of the couch. Something big.

Michael's chest clenched and he pulled the blanket tighter across his face.

It scurried around the couch, and as it passed alongside Michael, he saw long, spindly limbs pass by. Like a giant spider running along the floor.

Thump, thump. Thump, thump, thump.

He could just see matted black hair on the top of the thing's head—

The woman from the chimney.

She was running along the floor, and she was no longer small. Her frame was twisted and lengthened. The pale knobs that Michael was seeing were her elbows and knees—folded limbs that were now more than five feet long—as she scurried around on all fours.

Every muscle in Michael's body was tense, like he was trying to push his legs down into the couch and pull his arms up into his chest.

He could run back to his room, couldn't he? But the more Michael wished it the more helpless he felt—like the woman was already on top of him, pinning him to the couch, and Michael was too afraid to open his eyes and see her looming over him.

Faster and faster, she circled the couch, the knobs of her legs becoming a blur.

Thump, thump, thump, thump.

Then silence.

Out of the corner of his eye, Michael could see the knobs of her legs. Right next to him.

Michael's face twisted into a grimace, recoiling even before he saw the top of her head rising over the couch. Before he saw the twisted net of her hair part to reveal milky white eyes staring at him.

Chapter 13

Michael woke up to his Monday morning alarm—gasping—on the floor of his bedroom. He was still sitting at the foot of his bed, facing the bedroom door, revolver in hand.

It had just been a dream. The couch had been a dream.

But being terrified in his room, grabbing the revolver... that had been real.

Michael chuckled with relief. He was losing it.

He looked around at the food wrappers that littered the floor and the spilt bottle of rum...

At least he'd passed out safe.

He wiped the sleep from his eyes—then abruptly realized that the pistol was near his head with the safety off. He set the gun down to get his bearings.

Getting rid of the ring hadn't worked. The woman was still here—still in his chimney.

He had to go to work. How the Hell was he supposed to go to work after last night?

First, Michael looked under the door and waited. He couldn't see clearly under the bedroom door, but he should be able to see any shadows. And with his head to the floor, he should be able to feel or hear movement outside. He waited and waited.

When he was convinced that nothing was outside, he changed into his work clothes and psyched himself up to open the door. He kept the pistol ready in his right hand.

Michael grit his teeth and opened the door.

He surveyed the living room, but nothing had changed. The few blankets were amiss. The couch might've been pushed a little to the side, but he couldn't be sure.

The plastic container was knocked over, and the chimney was covered with sludge. Michael ignored it.

He shuffled his way along the living room wall, then slipped into the kitchen, keeping his eye on the chimney the entire time.

Michael grabbed an apple and a granola bar he had laying around and put them in his lunch bag. Then he grabbed his coat and was about to leave, but stopped. He took the pistol and stuffed it into the side of the shoe rack by the door. That way, he could grab it right away when he came home.

Then Michael went outside and waited on the porch for Colton to pick him up.

"Are you alright?"

Michael shook his head, more to wake himself up than to answer his boss. They were standing outside of a tenant house, looking at the undersized condenser unit out back. He felt sandwiched between the sun beating down on him and the hot air blowing off the unit.

"Michael, for Christ's sake, when's the last time you took a shower?"

"Four or five days ago."

He could see Colton out of the side of his vision, shaking his head.

"I'm taking you home after this job. You got to get some sleep *and* a shower."

Michael nodded.

He hadn't told his boss about what had been keeping him up at night. How could he? How in the Hell could he begin to explain it?

COLTON DROPPED HIM OFF after that job. Michael sat out front of his house and ate his lunch. He didn't want to go inside yet.

He was almost done when a police car pulled up in front of his house.

Michael swallowed, his throat suddenly very dry.

Two cops got out. Both were tall and thin, and regarded him from the street.

"Are you Michael Hitchens?" the first asked. He was an older Black man with a salt and pepper mustache.

"Yes, sir," Michael said from the step.

"We're here to talk to you about Jessica Smith. Can we come onto your property?"

Michael nodded and waited for them to approach.

The first introduced themselves as Officer Albrect.

The second, Officer Swain, was a young White woman, maybe younger than Michael was. She stood with her thumbs in her belt loops. Eyes narrowed at him.

"Have you heard from her?" Michael asked.

Officer Albrect hung his head for a moment, then pulled out a pad of paper and a pen.

"No, we haven't. No one has. When was the last time you saw Jessica?"

Michael felt like he'd been standing on a bridge that was now coming unraveled. Any hope that he'd hallucinated Jessica's disappearance came crashing down like a puppet with its strings cut.

On the front porch of his house, Michael told the officers about how Jessica had come over. How they had eaten spaghetti, how they'd slept together, and then gone to sleep together. Then how he'd woken up to find her gone.

In his blubbering, he even told them that Jessica had left her shoes.

"We had a good time," he muttered. "I don't know why she left."

"Breathe, son," Officer Albrect said. "Did she say anything, anything at all, that might be useful? Any new friends or other boyfriends?"

Michael just shook his head. He'd been over that night in his head... Jessica hadn't left him any clues.

But then, Michael already knew what happened to her.

A second, more immediate, realization was dawning on Michael at that moment: Jessica was gone, and Michael's house was the last place she'd been seen. Michael was the last person to speak to her.

"Michael," Officer Swain said suddenly. "Can we look around the place?"

Again, Michael nodded.

Swain walked off to look at the backyard, and as she rounded the side of the house, he saw her peek in the kitchen window. Then she disappeared around the corner.

Michael tried not to let worry show on his face. What if the police wanted to see the inside of his house? What if the Woman came out of hiding? ...What if she didn't? What had Michael left out that might incriminate him?

Officer Albrect cleared his throat and his mustache twitched. "Now, we have a few leads, and you're not a suspect. But... it would ease my conscience if you'd let us look around inside, too."

Michael's heart was pounding in his throat, and the words came out involuntarily. "Yes, sir."

Albrect chirped his walkie talkie. "Come on back, Swain. We're going to take a look inside."

With shaking hands, Michael unlocked and opened his front door, and the creak of the hinges broke the silence. He stepped inside and let the police pass.

And said a silent prayer that they didn't check the shoe rack.

Michael let them look over his dirty kitchen, as they stepped into the living room and whispered to themselves about muck pooled on and around the chimney. Held his breath while Swain tried to look up inside it and gave up because she didn't want to touch the black water. Let them go into his bedroom and bathroom.

All the while, Michael never took his eyes off the chimney.

"Thank you," Albrect said.

Michael startled. He didn't know how long the officer had been standing next to him.

"What's wrong with your chimney?" Officer Swain asked.

"It's, uh, leaking."

"You should get it looked at." She turned and left.

It was a ridiculous thought—that Michael didn't want the police to leave. He knew that, but it didn't stop him from thinking it. For what felt like the first time in weeks, Michael felt safe in his own home.

And now the police were leaving.

Michael would almost rather be locked up than stay here another night.

Officer Albrect stared at him. "I meant what I said. You're not a suspect, *right now*. I can't promise that won't change... Do me a favor: Don't leave town."

Michael said, "I won't. But... Can someone tell me if they find her? Please?"

Albrect paused as if he were choosing his words carefully. "Your best bet is to talk to Jessica's friend, Connie, since she was the one that helped file the report. I'll tell her you asked."

Michael watched them get in the police car and drive away. Tears streamed down his cheeks. He was too afraid to turn around, too afraid to run. He was too afraid to look in the chimney and find Jessica's body waiting for him.

And that's if he was lucky.

CHAPTER 14

MICHAEL STAYED IN HIS backyard again, drinking until the sun began to set. He would've stayed longer, but his phone was dying and his only chargers were for wall outlets.

There wasn't enough booze to numb the dread he was feeling.

Finally, he snuck inside, grabbed his pistol and a can of ravioli—one with a pull tab. Ran to his room and shut the door. Then he locked it and braced the chair against it again.

He slumped down on the floor and stayed there. Not even the pistol made him feel better. No amount of movies or mindless scrolling took his mind off of being trapped in his own room.

Michael dozed off several times, each time awakening suddenly. He was afraid to move from his vigilance on the floor. Afraid that he'd be taken unawares.

He was more afraid to dream.

Michael woke when it was absolutely and utterly dark. He was still laying on the floor at the end of his bed.

There were footsteps in the living room. Each step shook the floor and the bed. The thing lumbered to the door on all fours, its breathing heavy.

Michael had once seen a video of a bear pacing outside a camping tent. That was the image that came to mind now—something massive. Something hunting.

Michael tried to focus on the image of a bear because the other image was too horrific to contemplate.

Scraping came next—the sound of thick claws dragging across the door...

Reaching to the top of the door.

Michael craned his neck to follow the sound, and felt himself subconsciously shrinking lower, making himself small, hoping She would take pity on him and go away.

The Woman paced outside his door. Something rattled and fell off Michael's shelf, and broke on the floor.

Then the doorknob rattled, and She grabbed hold of it. He could just barely see it in the dark of the bedroom. It turned slowly and clunked heavily as it met the lock. Back and forth.

Clunk. Clunk...
CLUNK.

The gun was shaking in Michael's hands as he shrunk down to the fetal position. It was a pitiful comfort. It only held six bullets. There was no way six shots could stop whatever was behind the door—even if it was something that could be killed.

In that moment, Michael was so terrified that he thought to turn the gun on himself instead. At least that would work. At least then he wouldn't have to live in fear—wouldn't have to lose his sanity.

It was a long moment before he realized that the sounds had stopped. No more footsteps. No more doorknob rattling. No more heavy breathing.

Nothing from the living room.

She wasn't gone. Michael knew it.

From his position, lying on the floor, he tried to look under the bedroom door.

He saw four shadows—the shadows of four limbs.

She was waiting for him, crouched like a goddamn animal. Eyes unblinking. Waiting for him to open the door.

Waiting for him to fall asleep.

Then she would bust through the door, wrap her claws around his legs, and drag him away. Drag him up the chimney just like Jessica.

Michael wasn't sure if he slept.

Not until he heard a distant banging. Someone banging on his front door.

Michael looked around the room, illuminated by headlights from the driveway. The place was a mess. He'd pulled the covers off the bed at some point in the night; they were piled behind him. Trash wrappers littered the room.

He had four missed calls on his cellphone.

Michael called Colton.

"Jesus! Michael, I thought you were dead. Are you alright?"

"Yeah... I'm just not feeling well."

"You sound like shit. Are you... Yeah, take the day off. Hell, take the week off. Is there anything I can do for you? Want me to run to the grocery store?"

Michael looked at the bedroom door, uncertain whether the Woman was still lurking out there. Still waiting for him.

He imagined Colton coming in and getting dragged away.

"No!" The word came out in a hoarse whisper, and Michael added, "No. You don't want to catch what I've got. I'll... I'll call you if I need anything."

"Okay... Just, uh, take care of yourself."

Even the sun coming up didn't make Michael feel any better.

He grabbed an old backpack, and stuffed it with a week's worth of clothes, and grabbed snacks and chargers. He put the gun in his pocket.

For a moment, he considered grabbing toiletries before quickly abandoning the idea. He didn't have to go back out that way.

Then he opened his tiny bedroom window and stuffed the backpack through. With some effort, Michael climbed through after.

He couldn't stay here. He had to get away.

And that was exactly what he was going to do.

There was a little motel up the street. It was cheap and Michael had enough money saved that he could stay there at least a week. A week to figure things out. He'd be safe there. He could sleep and get a shower.

Michael grabbed his bag and ran to his car, but the door wouldn't open. He patted his pockets and realized—

He didn't have his keys.

They were inside. In the kitchen.

Slowly, Michael walked to the front porch, like a dead man walking to the firing squad.

He had a spare key. It was right there, in a magnetic box under the railing of the porch. Through the thin glass of the front door, he could see car keys and wallet sitting on his dining room table. And the edge of the living room beyond.

The only other option was to sneak back into his room and go the long way... Which wasn't really an option.

He wasn't going back into that living room.

Michael stooped down and grabbed the magnetic box with the spare key, legs feeling like they were fucking gelatin. He nearly cried when he saw the key was still there, and had to pull himself up with the railing.

Before he lost his nerve, Michael unlocked the front door and pushed it open.

Carefully, he peaked around the corners, making sure She wasn't waiting for him—hadn't been waiting for him all along.

It couldn't have been more than ten steps, but Michael was afraid to make any sound. He could barely hear anything over his own quivering breaths.

He was at the table, hand shaking as he slowly reached for the keys.

Thump.

Michael's eyes widened. He grabbed the keys and turned.

Thump, thump. Thump thump thump.

He sprinted for the door, each step felt like he was underwater as the footsteps grew quicker and louder behind him.

Thump thump thump THUMP THUMP THUMP

Michael barreled through the door, grabbed the pistol from his pocket, and whirled around—

In time to see a massive pale hand—fingers the length of fireplace pokers—snake around the corner to the living room and disappear from sight.

Michael fell to his knees, tears streaming down his face. Feverishly, he wiped them away—afraid to take his eyes off the doorway.

He stumbled forward and slammed his front door shut. Then he got in his car and drove away.

Chapter 15

Michael pulled into the *Crazy 8's* motel and sat in the car.

He couldn't get the image of Her out of his head. Every time Michael blinked, he saw the pale Woman from the chimney crawling through his house, over his things, clawing her way up the walls and around corners.

The gun was still beside him on the seat. Michael stuffed it in his side pocket. He had to keep it together—just a little while longer. Once he had a room, then he could sleep.

Sleep and forget about all of this.

He grabbed his bag and walked into the tiny lobby of the *Crazy 8.*

It was a dingy place that looked and smelled like it hadn't been updated since smoking inside was legal. At the moment, Michael couldn't give two shits about the place.

He waited at the front desk for a clerk to come around.

And waited.

The longer the moment dragged on, the more he expected the Woman to come out from the back room instead of a worker.

Would she follow him here? Could she do that?

Michael reached in his pocket and rested his hand on the pistol. The cold steel didn't comfort him at all.

Finally, an older lady came around to the front desk. She glanced at him and wrinkled her eyebrows before opening up a binder.

"We don't rent by the hour," she muttered.

At first, Michael didn't know what she meant, but then it dawned on him that he hadn't showered in days. He probably looked and smelled like a druggie.

"Do you have something for the week?" he asked.

Again, she gave him a curious glance.

"It's eighty a night."

Michael muttered okay, then handed her his credit card. She gave him the room key back and ushered him outside.

"It's on the end," she said, and left him.

Michael practically ran to the room.

MICHAEL LOCKED THE DOOR to his motel room, dropped his backpack on the ground, and collapsed on the twin bed.

He felt numb. Felt crazy.

Michael saw *Her*. Saw it—whatever that *thing* was.

She wasn't in his dreams anymore. The Woman in the chimney was real.

And he didn't know how to make her go away.

He laid back on the bed and fell asleep for an hour or so—blissful, dreamless sleep—before waking himself up.

He decided to shower. He stood there, letting the water run over him, and for a moment, it felt so good that it took his mind off of things.

For a moment.

Then he got dressed in fresh clothes and drove to the grocery store and bought enough canned ravioli and spaghetti to last him the week, and a box of donuts for good measure. Then he went to the liquor store and got enough beer to fill the fridge and enough rum that he wouldn't hopefully have to leave all week.

When he got back, Michael locked the door, turned on every light in the motel room, and started drinking.

MICHAEL KEPT DRINKING UNTIL he was having trouble walking straight. Not that he had to walk anywhere.

He watched TV and scrolled his phone, careful not to post anything while he was tipsy.

Michael checked Jessica's social media profiles. Each was tagged with comments praying for her and wondering why she hadn't responded. Michael didn't post anything. He was on the verge of tears just thinking about her.

Come to think of it, he'd cried more this week—out of sorrow and fear—than he'd cried in probably the rest of his life.

He hoped the cops didn't think he was hiding from them. Hoped they would find Jessica somewhere other than inside his chimney. Hoped that this whole horrific week had just been one long hallucination.

Michael thought about that last night with Jessica. How *he knew* that she'd fallen asleep next to him. How the sheets were pulled to the edge of the bed, like she'd been dragged out of bed by the Woman... Gods... dragged up the fucking chimney.

Michael tossed his phone off the bed—further than he'd meant to. He left it on the floor and grabbed the TV remote.

He didn't want to see anymore remnants of Jessica.

Michael turned on the TV and started on the first bottle of rum.

Rum helped. A little.

He put on an old stoner comedy, one that used to be funny back when Michael smoked pot, but that had lost its humor once he stopped. He was drunk enough to laugh at it, though.

And again, Michael found an escape. For a time.

As the scene went dark, Michael saw himself and the room reflected in the TV... But he swore that he saw someone else sitting beside him. Someone pale with long dark hair sitting beside him on the bed.

The scene changed again. It was the middle of the day in the movie and the stoner was lighting up.

And Michael swore he could feel someone sitting beside him on the bed.

He couldn't bring himself to turn and look.

He felt like a scared child hiding in his bed, thinking that the thin barrier of a blanket would save him.

When the scene went dark, Michael could see Her sitting beside him. See Her long dark hair—not her face—because she wasn't looking at the TV. She was staring at him.

The scene changed again, and the reflection disappeared, but Michael swore he could hear her raspy breaths. That he could feel hot breath on his neck.

She'd never left.

She was always there.

Michael woke up Tuesday morning. His head throbbed with pain—it was everything he could do to squint at the clock on the nightstand and check the time.

11:28 AM

He stumbled to the bathroom with his eyes half-closed and guzzled water from the sink. Then he grabbed his phone from the floor and sat on the edge of his bed.

It was only then that Michael froze and slowly looked around the room.

Mercifully, he was alone. Michael sighed with relief and cursed himself with his next breath. He should've brought Ibuprofen with him. Instead, he cracked open a beer and drank until his headache quieted down.

He had a missed call from his boss early that morning. No voicemail.

Hopefully, the old man got the hint that Michael wasn't coming into work today. Maybe he would take up Colton on the offer of taking the week off. Even though he'd gotten a room for the week, he hadn't sworn off going to work—if only to give him something to do.

When Colton called that afternoon, Michael was drunk enough to pick up the phone.

"Hey buddy, how are you holding up?"

"Oh just grand."

"That's some thick sarcasm."

"You could cut it like butter."

"Michael, are you drinking already?"

"Yep."

"...Maybe I should go."

"Maybe you should," Michael replied.

"Just take it easy. I've known you a long time... This ain't like you."

"Yeah? What do you know about me?

"Goodbye, buddy."

Michael dropped his phone on the bed, laid his head in his hands, and fought back a sob. He hadn't meant it like that. He hadn't.

It was just...

Michael didn't feel like he knew anything.

He didn't even know his house—his childhood house that he'd lived in all his life. There was a fucking monster living in it.

And it wouldn't let him go.

Chapter 16

TUESDAY PASSED IN HAZY snippets.

Michael indeed had enough canned food and liquor that he didn't have to leave the motel, but he didn't have enough to ease his worries.

Every time he woke up, the TV was still on—

And when the screen darkened, he could still see his reflection and the Woman sitting next to him. Saw her long hair blocking her face in the TV as she stared at him.

Could feel the depression next to him on the bed where she was sitting.

Saw her long hands and immense fingers. Even saw the black void in her face where a mouth should've been.

She wasn't really a Woman.

She never was.

Michael woke up in the motel still drunk.

It was Wednesday. He only knew because his phone told him so.

He sat there on the edge of the bed, staring at his socks that were now three days old. He should call someone, shouldn't he? He should at least call his sister.

In case he died here.

It was a morbid thought, but Michael didn't pause.

He scrolled through his contacts and found Ellie's number.

She would want to know. She would want to know.

"Hello, Michael?"

"Hi, sis."

"Did... did you just wake up? Shouldn't you be at work?"

"I took the week off."

"Oh. What's the occasion?"

"I just needed the time."

"Michael... Are you alright?"

Michael rubbed his face with his free hand. His breath was shaky. No, he wasn't fucking alright—it had been years since he'd been alright. Right now, he was losing his goddamn mind or being hunted by a monster.

But all that came out was a quiet, "No."

"Do you want me to come over?"

"No! I mean... No. I can't... Something's not right, Sis. I thought the ring was haunted, so I got rid of it, but... She's still here!"

"Wait, Michael, slow down. What do you mean? Grandma's ring? What do you mean you got rid of it?"

"I sold it."

"You what!"

"She's still here, Ellie—"

"I can't believe you! We ask so little of you because you can never be bothered to help out with anything. Uh, then you sold Grandma's engagement ring!" Someone else in the room talked, but Ellie cut them off too. *"Don't tell me to calm down, Darryl! He's fucking drinking again—Michael, listen, where did you sell the ring? We might still be able to get it back."*

"You're not listening to me—"

"You're right. Text me where you sold Grandma's goddamn ring. I don't want to talk to you anymore."

Ellie hung up, leaving Michael sitting on the bed with the phone in his hand. He tried desperately to keep staring at his own two feet and not the TV screen.

He could feel the Woman crawling across the bed to him.

MICHAEL WOKE UP WRAPPED in his sheets like a cocoon and staring up at the ceiling. Every light in the motel room was still on, but he could just see the edge of the nearby window and the darkness beyond.

He quickly turned away—fixing his gaze on the ceiling—and didn't dare look at the window again. Because he could see the reflection of the room in the window.

He wasn't alone.

The Woman from the chimney was running around the edge of the bed. Michael could just see the tips of her elbows and knees as she scurried around on the floor.

Thump thump thump thump thump.

Only now, the steps came quicker—

Michael saw legs—too many legs. Maybe eight. She walked around like a spider.

Each time she came to the side of the bed, the steps would pause. And Michael knew that she was looking at him with her milky white eyes and gaping mouth. But he was too afraid to look, too afraid to look and see just how many eyes were staring at him now.

Michael wept, his chest so tight he couldn't breathe.

She wouldn't touch the bed—God, why wouldn't She just take him? Why wouldn't She just drag him away like She did with Jessica?

Michael woke up to daylight. His head pounded, and the sheets were warm where he'd pissed himself. He was still cocooned in them... Just like his dream.

Michael unraveled himself and took a swig from the rum bottle to assuage his headache.

He sat on the edge of the bed, painfully aware that something was sitting beside him. He could feel the depression on the mattress. Could feel Her looking at him.

Michael stumbled to the bathroom while keeping his eyes on the floor.

If he just didn't look at her... maybe he was safe.

...Who was he kidding? He couldn't live like this.

He had to go back home and do... *something*. He couldn't just stay here and drink himself into a coma.

Michael took another swig of rum, then went to the bathroom and gave himself the world's most disheveled sponge bath, and changed into fresh clothes again.

He stuffed half a case of beer and the rest of the rum into his backpack with his chargers. Then he put the backpack in his trunk and—carefully—drove home.

MICHAEL PULLED INTO HIS driveway and sat in his car. At some point, he got out, grabbed his backpack of booze, rolled down the windows, and turned the car off.

He sat in the driveway, drinking the afternoon away, and trying to figure out what to do with himself. Trying to figure out if he really was at the end and ready to jump off the proverbial cliff.

Michael kept staring at the front door and at the windows to the kitchen. Nothing seemed out of the ordinary.

A knock on his car door startled him.

"Hey Michael, my man... What—what are you up to?"

Michael didn't have to look up at Felipe to see the confusion on his face.

"I don't want to go inside yet."

"Why not?"

"I just don't want to."

"Okay, okay. Well, you should take the keys out of the ignition, because there's some police officers two houses down. Don't want you to get in trouble."

Michael's hands went cold, but he nodded. He slid the key out and set it on the passenger seat.

Had they come back about Jessica? Were they in the neighborhood for some other reason?

"So where have you been, my man? Haven't seen you here the last couple days. Not like you to take off like that." Michael muttered something noncommittal, and Felipe kept talking. "Do you want me to watch the place for you? Keep an eye on things?"

"No."

"Oh. Okay, my man—Oh shit. They're pulling up."

Michael glanced lazily in the rear view mirror and saw the police cruiser pull in behind his car. He recognized both Officer Alberct and Officer Swain. She stood by the car while Officer Albrect approached the driver's side.

Albrect glanced inside the window as he passed.

"Step out of the car, please."

Michael tried to breathe evenly as he got out. He leaned on the door. "What's the problem, Officer?"

Albrect looked him over, his gaze lingering again on the booze in the car.

"Is there a reason you're not drinking in the comfort of your own home?"

"I... I just didn't feel like going inside... sir."

Albrect nodded, as if that was, in fact, as good a response as any. "Your sister, Ellie, asked us to come by and do a wellness check on you. Is there anything you want to talk about while myself and Officer Swain are here?"

Michael's throat felt so dry he could choke.

"No, sir."

Albrect sighed quietly. "Well, I can't let you keep drinking outside like this. So, I'm going to ask that you take your beer and whatever else you have with you back inside before you continue."

"I don't want to go inside."

"You either continue drinking inside or you'll be coming with us to the station."

Michael's eyes lingered on the front door of his house. He couldn't go back in there.

Maybe it would be better to go to the station. To get a drunk in public citation or whatever else they would lay on him. Hell—maybe it would be better to say he killed Jessica and go away.

Maybe the Woman in the chimney couldn't get him in jail.

"Excuse me, officer," Felipe said quietly. "I'll stay with him and keep an eye on him."

Michael looked at his neighbor weakly. He didn't have the strength to tell him no—not to worry about him.

Albrect shook his head. "He still has to go inside."

"Okay, okay. Come on, Michael. Let's get your stuff and go inside, huh? Thank you, Officer."

Michael felt numb to the world, like everything was far away. Felipe's voice sounded as if he was across the yard. The polices' conversation behind them sounded muffled. His own legs felt like they'd fallen asleep and he was walking on stumps. He clutched the half case of beer desperately—like at any moment it would fall out of his hands.

Michael looked hopefully at Felipe's house. Thought about the basement. It would probably be better to hide there with someone for company than to stew in his own filth back at the motel.

Michael stumbled forward, and strong hands guided him another way—

Across his driveway. Toward his front door.

"It's okay, Michael," Felipe said. "We'll get you inside and maybe see about some food."

Michael's head was shaking feebly—no, no, no. He was even mouthing the words, but no sound came out.

Felipe was behind him, so he couldn't see the sheer horror spreading across Michael's face as they stepped onto the porch. Felipe turned the knob and pushed open the door.

Then they stepped into Michael's house.

CHAPTER 17

MICHAEL STARED THROUGH THE kitchen as Felipe shut the front door behind them. Stared at the living room beyond.

"Here, buddy, I'll take that stuff," Felipe said, grabbing the box out of his hands.

Michael didn't move. He felt empty without having something to hold on to, so he crossed his arms and held his waist nervously.

Felipe glanced back a couple times, but pretended not to notice Michael's discomfort. He kept putting the drinks in the fridge.

Michael wasn't sure how long he'd been standing in the kitchen, but Felipe had started washing dishes. He was already making good time, halfway through loading the dishwasher.

"So, Michael... Are you going to sit down? ...Or are you going to stand there?"

Michael stood there, eyes focused on the living room. All he could see was the couch and the edge of the chair—he couldn't see the chimney.

But at least if he was standing by the door he could turn and run before the Woman got to him. He hoped.

"Hey, after the dishes, what else do you need me to do? I could help you pick up the place—something to take your mind off of things."

Maybe She would go after Felipe instead.

Michael felt ashamed merely thinking about it.

"Or we could put something on the TV," Felipe said, and start drinking. Or keep drinking, in your case."

Michael didn't answer.

Felipe finished washing the dishes and dried his hands.

"Okay, my man. Dishes are done. You finish up here, and I'm going to start in the living room."

Felipe had already turned and walked away before Michael realized where he was going.

Felipe disappeared around the corner of the living room. Then he was silent. No talking. No footsteps.

Michael felt like his heart had stopped and he couldn't breathe. He tried to call out for Felipe, but his voice came out a whisper.

"My man! Look at this! Did you know your chimney was leaking?" Felipe appeared, poking his head around the corner of the living room. "Do you have a mop bucket or something?"

"Closet," Michael muttered.

Felipe disappeared again, this time rummaging through Michael's closet. He walked past the doorway holding a small blue bucket, bottle of soap, and a pile of washrags.

Michael heard him fill the bucket from the bathroom tub, then heard him start scrubbing.

All the while, he was wondering when the Woman would come for him. When he would hear his neighbor scream in fright as she hauled him away or maybe in agony as she pulled him apart.

But it never came. She never came.

Felipe started humming.

MICHAEL INCHED HIS WAY closer to the living room.

All the while, Felipe kept cleaning the carpet around the chimney. He stopped twice to dump and refill the bucket of soapy water.

Michael's stomach was twisted with dread. What if Felipe couldn't see Her? Maybe she was invisible... Or maybe she was just waiting for Michael to come back—to taunt him by killing Felipe where Michael could see it...

Three times, Michael tried to call a warning to his neighbor—to tell him to get the fuck away from the chimney—but his voice was weak. Each time he could barely whisper Felipe's name, and never loud enough for Felipe to hear him.

What if She was waiting for Michael to try to warn him? What if Felipe was safe as long as Michael stayed quiet? As long as he suffered in silence and kept their little game going?

When Michael finally got to the threshold between the kitchen and the living room, Felipe was already halfway done cleaning the floor.

He was kneeling beside the chimney, touching it on occasion.

Michael's vision swam and he leaned on the wall.

Felipe looked up at him and paused. "There he is. Hey, this isn't too bad down here. Why don't you grab us some beers? I should be done in a few minutes."

Again, Michael felt a pit in his stomach, and he stared at his neighbor for a long moment before relenting. He went back to the kitchen, the entire time waiting for a scream that never came.

Michael grabbed an armful of beers and the half-bottle of rum. Then he sat the drinks on the small card table to the far side of the living room and sat so that he was facing Felipe and the chimney.

Michael cracked open a beer and continued his vigil.

IT WAS ANOTHER HALF an hour before Felipe finished cleaning the chimney.

In the end, he emptied the blue bucket of water, and set up a loud standing fan to dry the carpet—an old one that Michael usually stuck in the window in summertime to get a breeze.

Having the fan on settled Michael's nerves a bit. It was something akin to white noise. It helped him focus as Felipe sat down across from him at the card table.

"What do you say about dinner? You got something I can microwave? Cause I'm good with a lot of things, but I'm not such a good cook."

"Check the freezer."

Felipe left again and rifled through the freezer. Michael heard him unwrapping something—two somethings—and microwaving them one at a time.

The whole time, Michael's eyes didn't leave the chimney.

A few minutes later Felipe came back with sausage and egg breakfast sandwiches, and hot sauce for himself.

"You know, this will get us started. Then maybe I'll make some tater tots. Don't think I didn't notice those in there."

"Yeah."

Michael started to eat, and Felipe followed soon after. He had to admit, eating a warm meal, even a shitty breakfast sandwich, lifted his spirits.

Both men ate in silence and finished quickly.

Felipe pushed aside his paper plate and trash. "Man, are you finally going to tell me what's eating you? Cause something clearly isn't right."

Michael's eyes flickered between his neighbor and the chimney.

"I think you were right about the ring... my grandmother's ring."

"What do you mean?"

"I've been... seeing things. I, uh, I got rid of the ring the other day. I thought that might fix things. But I don't think it did."

Felipe rubbed his chin in confusion.

"Did you mean what you said?" Michael asked, voice cracking. "About horrible shit finding us and not letting go?"

"Michael, man, I'm sorry. I know you've been going through a lot recently. I shouldn't—shit—I shouldn't have said that stuff about the ring."

"But do you believe that?"

"I do believe that. I mean, I think I heard the line in a movie, but this is probably..." Felipe shook his head and then met Michael's eyes with a sadness and a seriousness the neighbors hadn't shared before. "Have you seen a doctor, Michael?"

Michael smirked. "No. It's not like that. I'm not crazy..."

"It couldn't hurt, right? Hey, if I'm sick, I go to a doctor. If my car isn't running right, I go to a mechanic. If my AC is broken, I call the HVAC guys. If my lawn needs mowing, my wife gets me to do it."

Michael chuckled awkwardly, more so because Felipe was chuckling awkwardly than because of the joke he'd made.

"I might have something," Felipe said. "My wife, she likes these documentaries about mastering yourself and stuff. We should try this one thing: Mastering your fear."

Michael shrugged. "Fuck it. Okay." What did he have to lose?

"Okay, so, remember that I'm here with you. Describe the ghost to me and describe when things started getting bad for you. Do that, and getting it out in the open will give you power over your fear." Then he squinted at Michael. "But you should probably also see a doctor, or a, uh, shrink when you can. Cause they're the professionals, you know."

Michael glanced at the chimney—clean and empty.

"I saw her in my dreams, at first. She was kind of wispy and thin, and pale. Her hair was long and dark. She always wore this white nightgown-type dress.

"But even when I first saw her, I knew something wasn't quite right. The more I saw her, the more she... changed. I couldn't tell what was wrong, but her face would be too long, her eyes white and her mouth black. Her hands were too long, her fingers...

"I, uh, couldn't really sleep after a while. I started drinking more to get to sleep. It helped, a little. But she's been hounding me. Stalking me."

Felipe was leaning forward, listening intently. "Like she's following you around? Not just in your dreams?"

Michael didn't answer at first because across the room, the chimney started leaking black water. It was pooling on the bricks.

How long had it been leaking? Had he not noticed because the fan was so noisy?

"Yeah," he muttered. "Now she's not even human anymore... She's a monster..."

Long fingers of a massive hand snaked out from the chimney, wrapping around the bricks. Dark, matted hair fell out as *She* pulled her way out of the chimney.

"Oh fuck," Michael whined. Tears welled up in his eyes and he looked down at the table—part in shame, mostly in terror.

Felipe reached across the table and grasped Michael's hand. "It's okay, Michael. I'm here. This is the first step to mastering your fear."

Another hand snaked its way out of the chimney. Then another, and another. Pale fingers the length of fireplace pokers wrapped around the bricks, like a dozen giant spiders crawling out.

A twisted face peaked from the chimney. Veins ran through her milky eyes like cracked eggs.

Michael looked away and found himself looking into Felipe's eyes.

"Just breathe," Felipe said. "Breathe and look at me. The first part is accepting your fear."

Michael was too afraid to nod. His breath was coming in shallow gasps. Sweat beaded on his face. He stared at Felipe while he talked, but watched the horror unfolding from the corner of his eye.

The Woman pulled herself out of the chimney, long body slithering free like a snake. She moved carefully. Deliberately. And when Her body was entirely free of the chimney, Michael wondered how the Hell she fit up there in the first place.

Her body and limbs were so long that She couldn't stand up in the house, so she crawled on a dozen legs. Her white dress was tattered and torn, draped across a pale, worm-like body—shredded like spider webs.

Her face was the most human part of Her. Two white eyes stared at Michael. Her mouth was the color of utter darkness and it hung open all the way to the floor, dripping like a black waterfall.

She crept forward, legs moving like a disjointed clock. She crept.

Behind her, black water trickled out of the chimney—

And Felipe didn't turn. Didn't hear because the fan was so loud!

Michael's heart was pounding so fast and so hard, his throat clenched so tight that he was choking himself—it felt like the Woman already had one hand, maybe three, wrapped around his neck.

"It's okay, Michael," Felipe said, squeezing his clammy hand. "It's okay."

All the while, She crept like a gargoyle across the living room. Eyes unblinking, mouth hanging open. With every step, she pinned hair to the floor and tore it free, sending tufts of black tumbling to the carpet and mixing with the ink pouring from her mouth.

The water from the chimney began to pour.

The smell of mildew and rot grew overpowering, and for the first time, Felipe stopped reassuring him and wrinkled his nose.

"You should get that chimney checked out, Michael."

For the first time, Michael looked away from Felipe.

Looked at Her.

Her face was hanging in the air over Felipe's right shoulder. The rest of her body was slithering and crawling to catch up. It pooled beneath her, coiling around on itself.

She was staring at Michael. Unblinking.

Michael quivered, shaking his head in the smallest movements, pleading silently with a monster not to take him.

"It's okay, Michael—"

But as Felipe spoke, he turned—looking over his left shoulder, toward the kitchen, and coughed. He didn't see Her.

Then Felipe turned the other way.

The Woman pounced on top of Felipe, knocking him, the chair, and the table over, leaving Michael alone. The house shook, pictures falling from the wall and shattering. Her body contorted so that all the dozens of her hands and dagger-like fingers could grab him.

Felipe screamed, and it was cut short. Enormous hands wrapped around his torso, his face, his arms and legs. She squeezed and bones snapped.

But for a moment—only a moment—She wasn't looking at Michael.

The sounds stopped. She released her grip, and Michael's neighbor slumped into a lifeless pile.

She wrapped one enormous hand around Felipe's mangled leg and dragged him backward. Now Her steps were slow and heavy, and he felt the house rattling under Her every step.

Michael was afraid to move. Afraid to turn. Afraid to run or even breathe.

He was watching Felipe. His neighbor's body looked like a stained cloth doll—his skin already turning horrible shades of purple. Blood trickled from his mouth, his ears, and his eyes…

Felipe's eyes flicked between the monster dragging him and Michael, who stared back.

Felipe was still alive. His face twisted into a silent scream, mouth slack.

The Woman slithered and folded herself back up inside the chimney. Black water was pouring out, running down her pale skin and matted hair.

She stared at Michael all the way until her face vanished behind the bricks. She pulled Felipe up at last, his bones crunching as he went.

Felipe stared at Michael until he disappeared into the chimney.

Chapter 18

Michael turned and sprinted to his room. Locked the door. Shoved the chair under the knob. Toppled shelves and dressers over in front of the door. Pushed his bed against the pile.

Then he curled up against the back wall, sobbing and hysterical.

Felipe was gone. Jessica was gone.

Every time Michael closed his eyes, he saw flashes of their faces as they were hauled up into the chimney.

He scrambled for a bottle of rum. There was only a mouthful left. Empty cans of beer lay scattered on the floor.

There was nothing left to numb him. Nothing left to save him. In his gut, Michael knew that no amount of shit piled against the door would save him. No amount of running or hiding in the motel would save him.

He curled back against the wall, sobbing until his chest and stomach cramped, until his face was numb and tears didn't come anymore.

Michael hadn't heard the Woman crawl back out of the chimney. He only knew She was there because of the scraping at the door. Her long fingers scraping the wood and rattling the feeble pile bracing it.

Occasionally, the doorknob rattled.

WHEN SHE CAME FOR him, Michael was no longer sure if he was still awake or if he was dreaming.

Even inside the house, Michael knew the Woman was much bigger than She seemed. She crawled across the living room, Her crooked elbows scraping the ceiling, legs multiplying as she advanced. She walked on twelve legs, thirty, then hundreds. The limbs twisted and intertwined so tightly together that they looked like a web—

She was a torso—a body—draped in pale cloth, hung in the center of the web.

Her slack-jaw yawned, dripping black across the room. It widened, running together with her hair, stretching until Michael could no longer see the ends of it—sprawling like a black sea.

Her eyes grew, looking down on Michael with absent, arid judgment, of endless millennia, of rotten indifference. Pale sickness blurred together until she's a single white sun floating above a black world.

The sky was filled with legs, with hair—

With cracks.

Michael lulled on the floor, half-immersed in his nightmare, half-aware that the Woman was standing over him.

She pushed through the door. Merely pushed. The door and frame tore like paper. All his piled things gave way like a stack of toys.

A mere fragment of Her stood over him, dripping black water, tongue long enough to reach out to him. The rest of Her hung in Michael's nightmare.

The piece of Her grabbed his ankle and dragged him through the door and across the living room. It felt like a cold vice around his leg.

Michael didn't fight. Didn't scream.

He'd been a child playing with a flashlight, and who'd just accidentally seared his eyes by looking into the sun.

He looked absently around the room as She dragged him. Watched as his world fell away.

Even when Michael looked upon the piece of Her, saw her milky white eyes and yawning black mouth, he didn't scream. In that moment, the fragment of Her didn't look half as scary as the real thing.

He felt the hard brick of the fireplace beneath his hips, then his back, head, and arms. Cold black water trickled under his clothes. His head fell slack as She hauled him up into the chimney. His other leg snapped as She pulled him through.

The chimney narrowed, and Michael was scraped raw as his lifeless body was dragged up and up—

Far higher than his chimney had actually been.

The stained bricks of the opening grew smaller and smaller, shrinking until they were no more than a saucer, no more than a pinprick... until the light was gone completely.

Michael felt nothing but the scraping bricks and Her cold hand around his ankle.

He didn't know how long had passed, but the chimney began to fill with light. She was pulling him toward an opening.

Toward a crack.

Only then did Michael scream.

END

THANK YOU FOR READING

I HOPE YOU ENJOYED reading this story as much as I enjoyed writing it. If you did, I would greatly appreciate a short review on Amazon or your favorite book website. Reviews are crucial for any author, and even just a line or two can make a huge difference.

Try these unsettling stories

Acknowledgments

Thank you, Mom, for getting me started on horror.
Thank you, Ren, for rekindling that curiosity.

About Author

If you want to stay up to date on the latest about Samuel's publishing news and blog, check out his website and consider signing up for his monthly newsletter.

www.SamuelFlemingBooks.com

Samuel can also be found on Reddit, Tiktok, and Facebook.

Samuel Fleming is a Science Fiction and Fantasy author.

He grew up in Maryland, spending most of his time swimming and writing. Swimming gave him a lot of time to daydream, so the two hobbies complemented each other well. Idle day dreams turned into stories, some of which stuck with him for years. These days he swims a little less and writes a lot more.